Ed stopped suddenly under a tree, and Perdita went a few steps out of the shelter of the umbrella before she realized he wasn't beside her, and retraced her steps.

"Is something the matter?"

"Yes."

"What is it?"

"I don't think," Ed said slowly, "that I can go any farther until I've kissed you."

The last of the breath she had been so carefully hoarding leaked out of Perdita at that, and she looked at him, her heart hammering so loudly she was sure he must hear it. The smack of it against her chest wall was really quite painful, and she swallowed carefully.

"I …I'm not sure that's a good idea," she managed with difficulty.

"Nor am I," said Ed. "But let's try, and then we'll know."

One hand still holding the umbrella above their heads, he drew Perdita toward him with the other. It would have been easy for her to sidestep him, to pull back, but she didn't. She couldn't resist this deep, dark pull of attraction any longer, and she didn't want to. Just one kiss, she told herself hazily. That wouldn't be so bad, would it?

Dear Reader,

Just as the Harlequin Romance® line has changed over the years to reflect changes in the reality of women's lives and expectations, so my own books have evolved, over the twenty years I've been lucky enough to write for Harlequin, to reflect changes in my own life.

My stories are always drawn in some part from either my own experiences or those of my friends, and this is particularly true of *Promoted: to Wife and Mother*. It's one of the best things about writing romance. We can't always control what happens when we face difficult situations in real life, but when it's your story, you can make sure it has a happy ending!

I think we all know things don't always work out the way they should, but it's nice to think that sometimes, to a heroine we can all identify with, they just *might*....

Jessica Hart

JESSICA HART
Promoted: to Wife and Mother

HARLEQUIN®

TORONTO • NEW YORK • LONDON
AMSTERDAM • PARIS • SYDNEY • HAMBURG
STOCKHOLM • ATHENS • TOKYO • MILAN • MADRID
PRAGUE • WARSAW • BUDAPEST • AUCKLAND

ISBN-13: 978-0-373-17501-7
ISBN-10:   0-373-17501-9

PROMOTED: TO WIFE AND MOTHER

First North American Publication 2008.

Jessica Hart was born in West Africa, and has suffered from itchy feet ever since, traveling and working around the world in a wide variety of interesting but very lowly jobs, all of which have provided inspiration to draw from when it comes to the settings and plots of her stories. Now she lives a rather more settled existence in York, U.K., where she has been able to pursue her interest in history, although she still yearns sometimes for wider horizons. If you'd like to know more about Jessica, visit her Web site, www.jessicahart.co.uk.

Selected praise for Jessica:

"Jessica Hart is a marvel."
—*Romantic Times BOOKreviews*

"Jessica Hart delivers delightful reading, creating intense characters and an intriguing premise."
—*Romantic Times BOOKreviews*

"One of Harlequin Romance's brightest stars!"
—*CataRomance.com*

Jessica's next fresh and vibrant story is out in July:
Newlyweds of Convenience

CHAPTER ONE

PERDITA drummed her fingers on the sleeves of her jacket and tried not to look as if she were sulking. What a waste of time this so-called leadership development course was turning out to be! So far all she had done was spend hours filling out a questionnaire in the expectation that she would turn out to be a dolphin—warm, friendly, expressive—only to be informed that in spite of answering every question in a carefully dolphinesque way, she was in fact an attention-seeking peacock.

A *peacock*!

And, just to add to her humiliation, it appeared that she was the *only* peacock. Everybody else got to be a jolly, sociable dolphin or a nit-picking owl—not that Perdita would have wanted to be one of *them*—while she was left in the corner on her own.

She had known this course was a mistake. Not wanting to look as if she were envying the dolphins, who were all bonding madly and agreeing with each other in the corner, Perdita inspected her nail polish for chips instead, and was momentarily distracted in admiration of the colour.

Vixen, it was called. Now *that* was what she called a colour to be reckoned with. But the deep red might have been a give-away, she realised belatedly. The female dolphins probably stuck to a non-threatening pale pink and, as for the owls, they would be too busy checking their spreadsheets to even think about painting their nails.

Perdita sighed, tucked her hands away and started tapping a foot instead.

'It looks like we're the only two on our own. Do you think that means we belong together?'

Turning sharply, Perdita found herself looking into a pair of amused grey eyes, and she was conscious of a tiny jolt of recognition. It was the man who had arrived late the night before.

He had missed dinner and the introductory briefing, but she had noticed him later in the bar, although for the life of her Perdita hadn't been able to work out why. It wasn't as if he were particularly striking or different in any way. He was just a man—not particularly tall, not particularly handsome, not particularly anything.

Perdita couldn't understand why she had noticed him at all.

She had been in the centre of a group who were definitely having the best fun, but he hadn't made any attempt to come over and join them. Instead he had talked for a while with a quiet group of people—owls, probably—before disappearing and leaving Perdita feeling unaccountably piqued at his lack of interest.

But now here he was.

She studied him with interest. Up close, he was a lot less ordinary than he had appeared across the bar. The grey eyes were very keen, and creased with a fan of laughter lines, she couldn't help noticing. She was always a sucker for those. The hint of humour made an intriguing contrast with his austere features and that firm, not to say stern, mouth.

Hmm. Not gorgeous, not even *that* attractive, taken bit by bit, Perdita decided, but she was uneasily aware that her hormones, which had been in hibernation since Nick had broken her heart, were definitely stirring.

Unaccountably ruffled by her reaction to him, Perdita put up her chin. 'You don't belong with me unless you're a peacock,' she told him and her bright brown gaze skimmed over his grey jumper and black trousers. 'And I have to say that you don't look like one to me!'

The corner of his mouth twitched in acknowledgement of his apparent lack of flair. 'No, I'm not a peacock. Apparently I'm a panther,' he said. His face was completely straight, but the grey eyes gleamed in a way that made Perdita feel quite…*funny*…

'Really?' she said, wondering if he were joking. According to the bumph they had been handed that morning, panthers were typical alpha males: forceful, decisive, ambitious and more than a little ruthless, and Perdita hadn't been at all happy to discover that she was not just an attention-seeking peacock, but she also had a strong panther ascendant. Talk about an unappealing combination!

'I wouldn't have put you down as a panther,' she told him honestly.

Although, on second thoughts, there was something about his mouth that made her think he probably wasn't someone to mess with.

'That'll be my strong owl ascendant confusing you,' he said and Perdita laughed.

'Ah, so when you're not prowling around dominating everyone, you're poring over your spreadsheets and double-checking your calculations?'

'While you peacocks hold court in the bar,' he agreed suavely.

Perdita looked at him sharply, but it was impossible to tell whether he had noticed her last night after all, or was simply picking an easy example of what peacocks might do.

'I wanted to be a dolphin,' she confessed, just trace of sullenness in her voice, and he raised an eyebrow.

'Why?'

'*Why?*' she echoed incredulously. 'It's obvious, isn't it? Everybody *loves* dolphins. I don't see why I'm not one, in fact,' she grumbled. 'I filled out the form really carefully. I was sure I'd be a dolphin. I mean, I'm friendly, aren't I? I can do all that team stuff they're supposed to be so good at.'

'Dolphins are very patient and relaxed,' he pointed out, and Perdita bridled.

'*I'm* relaxed! I'm more relaxed than anyone! *And* I can be patient.'

In reply, he looked down to her pointy suede boots. One was tapping the floor and, as Perdita followed his gaze, she stopped it abruptly and jerked her foot back.

'I'm just bored,' she told him crossly. 'I've had enough of standing here on my own while those owls and dolphins sit around bonding and congratulating each other on being good team members!'

She eyed the group of dolphins in the far corner sourly. 'Look at them, all eek-eeking to each other! Any minute now they'll be balancing balls on their nose and clapping their flippers.'

Her companion laughed. 'You are *definitely* not a dolphin,' he told her. 'If ever I saw a peacock, it's you!'

Perdita scowled. 'And you would know so much about this because…?' she asked sarcastically.

'I'm observant.'

A smile hovered around his mouth as he studied Perdita, her slender figure quivering with annoyance. Even if she hadn't been banished to a corner on her own, she would have stood out in the room—in any room, he decided.

Although not strictly pretty, she was immaculately groomed, but it wasn't her looks that drew the eye. Instead, there was a vibrancy about her, a forcefulness of personality that was evident in the generous mouth, the lively planes of her face and the dark, sharp eyes, in the quick gestures and the way she threw back her head and laughed.

'I saw you in the bar last night,' he told her. 'You had the biggest group around you and you were making them all laugh. And this morning, at breakfast, no one was really talking until you came in and sat down. You were the one who broke the ice when they were handing out the questionnaires.'

'There you are,' said Perdita, not quite sure whether to be pleased that he had noticed her after all or put out at the faint undercurrent of laughter in his voice that suggested he found her somehow amusing. 'That proves I'm a dolphin, surely? I was being fun and friendly…those are dolphin character-istics,' she pointed out.

'Yes, but a dolphin just likes to play along with everyone else. That's why they're all getting on over there,' he said, fol-lowing her gaze to the group in the corner, who did indeed seem to be having a much better time than the owls at the other end of the room. 'But, if you were in that group, you wouldn't just sit there being like everyone else. You'd be dominating it completely, and the group dynamics would be quite different.'

'I would *not* dominate it!' Perdita's dark eyes sparkled with temper.

'Oh, yes, you would,' he said coolly. 'They would all be laughing and having fun, but you would be the one making it happen, and making sure that they were all looking at *you*.'

Perdita eyed him with dislike. She didn't want to admit

that there was a certain familiarity about the scenario he had just described. It wasn't a comfortable feeling to think that a perfect stranger could see through her quite so easily.

'How come you know so much about it, anyway?' she demanded.

He shrugged. 'I'm interested in people.'

'That's not very panther of you,' she said waspishly, and he grinned, a surprising smile that made him look suddenly younger.

'All right, I'm interested in getting the most out of the people who work for me,' he conceded.

'That sounds more like it,' sniffed Perdita, who was still feeling oddly jolted by the suddenness of his smile. It had really been quite startling to see how completely it transformed him, and then was gone again. 'You seem very well-informed,' she added with just a trace of sarcasm. 'Have you been on courses like this before?'

'A few,' he said carelessly. 'What about you?'

'No, this is my first.'

'You surprise me. Most firms take management training seriously these days.'

'My ex-boss didn't think they were worth spending any money on. There was talk about an assertiveness course a couple of years ago, but my colleagues threatened to strike if I was allowed to go on it. The feeling was that if I were any more assertive than I already was I would be unbearable. All nonsense, of course,' said Perdita, who had told this as a story against herself often enough now to be able to treat it as a joke just as everyone else did.

Almost.

The man didn't laugh. 'You might have found it useful,' he said.

'I doubt it,' she said airily. 'I've got no time for these courses, to be honest. I think they're all a waste of time. I've got far too much to do to be messing around with all this nonsense about peacocks and panthers. What's the point of it all?'

She hadn't really meant it as more than a rhetorical question, but the man replied anyway.

'It's about leadership, isn't it?' he said. 'The idea is that you can lead a team more effectively if you're aware of the different personality types and can recognise the different strengths each individual can bring to a particular task. An effective leader is one who is able to create an environment in which everyone can contribute to the best of their ability. It's not about one type being better than another. Ideally you need a range of personality types on your team—but only if you can identify the strengths and weaknesses of each, and get everyone working together rather than at cross-purposes.'

'You're obviously a convert,' said Perdita, her wide mouth turning down dismissively.

'And you're not?'

'I don't think that discovering that I'm a peacock or whatever is going to make any difference to the way I work, certainly,' she told him. 'I do my job, and I do it well. I tell my staff what to do and they do it. How much more leadership do they need?'

'And then you wonder why you're not a dolphin,' he murmured. 'Is it possible that you have a panther ascendant instead?'

How had he guessed *that*? Perdita gave him a hostile look. She didn't have to admit anything. 'It's all rubbish, anyway,' she grumbled, avoiding a direct answer, but there was a gleam in his eyes that suggested he might have a pretty good idea about what it would have been in any case.

'Then what are you doing here?' he asked.

'I've got no choice,' she said. 'The board have just appointed a new chief executive, some pretentious City hot shot who wants to impress us all with his forward thinking.' Perdita snorted. 'I think it's all a lot of nonsense. The famous Edward Merrick hasn't bothered to come and meet the workforce yet, but he's already decided that all his executives will benefit from three days messing around in the Lake District.'

'You don't sound very impressed by him.'

'Oh, I dare say he knows his stuff,' Perdita acknowledged. 'He's got a great track record in turning companies around,' she admitted grudgingly.

'Then what's the problem?'

'I just think he should find out what's happening on the ground before he starts swanning in and changing everything. OK, so the old chief executive lost his grip in the end, but the company is strong in lots of ways and frankly I've got better things to do than pander to a lot of fads about leadership.'

She pushed her hair behind her ears in an unconscious gesture of frustration. 'Quite apart from anything else,' she told him, 'it's really inconvenient timing—not that there's ever a time when we *aren't* busy in Operations. I keep thinking of all the work piling up when I'm away. I spent half the night catching up with emails as it is.'

Perhaps 'half the night' was a bit of an exaggeration, Perdita admitted to herself, but she *had* had to plug in her laptop and get on with some work. She couldn't afford to treat these few days away like a total jolly, whatever some people—unspecified, she added mentally with a dark look at her companion—might think about her propensity for propping up the bar. She was a professional, after all, and it was obviously time to make sure that he knew it.

'I'm Perdita, by the way,' she said, offering her hand. 'Perdita James. I'm Operations Manager for Bell Browning Engineering.'

He took her hand and smiled at her. 'Ed Merrick,' he said.

For a moment she was too taken up with the feel of his fingers wrapped firmly around hers to take in what he had said, but when the name finally registered Perdita's carefully professional smile froze.

'Ed?' she echoed in a hollow voice, carefully withdrawing her hand. 'Er…would that be Ed as in Edward, by any chance?'

'Ed as in pretentious City hot-shot,' he agreed equably.

Excellent. Perdita stifled a sigh. How to get off on completely the wrong foot with your new boss in one easy lesson by Perdita 'Big Mouth' James.

Her heart sank as she considered her options. She could fall back on the tried and tested technique of joking her way out of trouble, or she could make a grovelling apology.

Glancing at him, she was relieved to glimpse a glint of what she hoped was amusement in the grey eyes. Thank goodness he appeared to have a sense of humour! Grovelling wasn't really her style, anyway.

So she leant forward confidingly. 'I always think that if you're going to have a good relationship, it's best to start with an insult and then things can only get better,' she said straight-faced.

'Well, that's one way of looking at it,' said Edward Merrick, his look of amusement deepening. 'I heard that you were famous for straight-talking,' he went on, 'but I hadn't expected a practical demonstration quite so soon, I must admit!'

'You mean you knew who I was all along?' Perdita demanded, stiffening.

'I've seen your CV,' he said, 'complete with a photograph that doesn't do you justice at all.'

'You should have told me who you were!' Embarrassed at having been caught in unprofessional behaviour, Perdita characteristically went on the offensive. She was *very* glad that she hadn't grovelled now! 'I had no idea that you were going to be here. We thought there would just be the six of us.'

She looked over to where her colleagues were busy being owls, except for the head of Human Resources, who was a dolphin, of course. Had any of them realised that their new boss was among them? Surely one of them would have said if they had? She would have to warn them all off when they broke for coffee.

'We were told that you wouldn't be able to come,' she added severely, glancing back at Edward Merrick, as if her indiscretion in describing her new boss to a perfect stranger was somehow his fault.

'I didn't think I was going to be able to make it,' he said. 'Things were getting very complicated on the home front, but there was a last minute change of plans so I booked myself in at the last minute.'

'Without telling us?'

'I imagine you were all on your way here before I decided,' he said by way of an apology. 'I just got in the car and drove up from London. It meant that I missed the original briefing and had no chance to introduce myself to you all over dinner. I was hoping to get a chance to do that this morning, but there hasn't been any free time yet.'

'And that wouldn't have been nearly as much fun as letting us all make complete fools of ourselves first,' said Perdita bitterly.

'I haven't met any of the others yet,' said Ed. 'For the

record, I would have preferred to have met you all on your home ground, but this course comes highly recommended, and it doesn't run again until the autumn, so I wanted to get everyone on it now if possible. And, when I thought about it, it seemed like a good opportunity for us to get to know each other before I move to Ellsborough permanently. That's why it was worth my while to drive all the way up from London at the last minute.'

'Oh, and I'm so glad you did!' Perdita didn't bother to disguise her sarcasm. 'It's just what I wanted, a chance to humiliate myself completely in front of my new boss!'

The corner of his mouth twitched. 'I'd have known what you thought anyway,' he pointed out. 'You peacocks aren't very good at disguising your feelings.'

'Still, it was rude.' Gritting her teeth, Perdita made herself apologise. 'I'm sorry, I shouldn't have said that about you being pretentious.'

'Don't worry about it,' he said with a shrug. 'You don't get to be a panther without developing a very tough skin! Ah, good,' he interrupted himself as there was a general movement at the other end of the room. 'It looks as if something is happening now…'

Sure enough, the course facilitators were beginning to divide everybody up into groups and Perdita found herself separated from Edward Merrick.

Just as well, she thought, torn between relief and chagrin. She couldn't believe what a mess she had made of her first meeting with him! It wasn't that she had ever had any intention of grovelling to him, but it irked her that she had been betrayed into those careless remarks. Perdita had always prided herself on her professionalism and she was mortified at the idea of not appearing at her best.

Of course, Ed Merrick would probably say that was the peacock in her. What a lot of rubbish *that* was!

Determined to prove him wrong about her, Perdita resolved to sit quietly in her group and let everyone else do the talking this time. If Ed cared to glance her way, he would see that she wasn't showing off, but blending in perfectly with all the owls and dolphins.

Unfortunately, she hadn't taken into account just how uncomfortable it was for her to sit in silence. Everyone in the group had been given a few strips of paper each and there was an awkward pause as it became clear that they were going to have to work out the task themselves.

OK, she could do this, Perdita told herself, shifting uneasily. She would show Edward Merrick. She *wouldn't* be the first to speak. She would let someone else take the lead.

But the silence was so oppressive that she couldn't resist murmuring an aside about the facilitator to her neighbour, who started to laugh, and before she knew quite how it happened the rest were joining in an animated conversation. They had to be reminded of their task by the facilitator and, forgetting that she was supposed to be taking a back seat, Perdita was the first to lean forward with a suggestion.

After that, the ideas started coming thick and fast. 'Wait, wait, wait!' she cried, waving her hands around. 'Slow down, people! We need to keep track of all this. Andy, why don't you be chair?'

They were discussing the best way to proceed when Perdita happened to glance across at the neighbouring group, which just happened to include Ed Merrick, who just happened to look up at the same time. The cool grey gaze encompassed the animated group around Perdita and he smiled knowingly as his eyes met hers, and she flushed, knowing exactly what he was thinking.

What was it he had said? *If you were in that group…you'd be dominating it completely…making sure that they were all looking at you.*

Tilting her chin, she jerked her gaze crossly away. She had just wanted to get things happening or they would be here until teatime. Huffily, she tried to concentrate on the task in hand, but it wasn't that challenging and, in spite of herself, her eyes kept wandering back to Ed's group.

A panther like him was a fine one to talk about dominating! It was easy to see who was leading *that* group, although Perdita struggled to work out exactly how he was doing it. He wasn't showing off or being loud or forceful or saying very much at all, in fact, but there was no question that Ed was the centre of his group quite as much as she was of hers.

It puzzled Perdita. She was very conscious of her own stylish outfit, painted nails and lipstick. The other women had gone for a much more casual look, but Perdita didn't do casual—never had and never would. So perhaps it was inevitable that she should stand out within her group, but Ed had no such excuse. He was just sitting there, wearing that dull grey top with the sleeves carelessly pushed up his forearms. He wasn't taller or better-dressed or better-looking than the others, but there was just something about him that made him stand out.

Studying him surreptitiously, Perdita could see the way the others in his group were deferring to him, but it didn't make sense. If he were really the panther he claimed to be, shouldn't he be riding roughshod over them all? Instead he seemed to be dominating the group by not doing very much at all.

The more she watched him over the day, though, the more

Perdita recognised a quiet but steely strength to him that translated as a natural *gravitas*, a quality as unmistakable as it was hard to define. Ed didn't need to snarl to control a situation, it seemed, and, although he was hardly prowling, he held himself with an enviable assurance that put her in mind of a big cat's leashed power.

Maybe there was something pantherish about him after all, Perdita decided. It was lucky that he had told her about his owlish streak, or she might have had to be impressed. As it was, whenever she remembered the glimmer of amusement in his expression as he had told her about his owl ascendant, part of her wanted to laugh, while another part would squirm uneasily at the memory of the humorous gleam in his eyes and that unexpected smile.

She couldn't even accuse Ed of being standoffish. As soon as she could, she had warned her colleagues that their new boss was among them, which meant that they, at least, were able to make a good impression on him. Perdita saw him talking to them all at one time or another, but he never made any effort to talk to her again. Perhaps it wasn't that surprising after she had accused him of being pretentious, but she couldn't help feeling a little miffed that he appeared to have dismissed her already.

The hotel was out in the wilds of the Lake District and after dinner there was nothing to do but head for the bar. A natural extrovert, Perdita was on sparkling form, but Ed was clearly unimpressed by her social skills, treating her on the few occasions their paths crossed that evening with a kind of amused detachment that left Perdita's peacock feathers distinctly ruffled.

Some people were intimidated by her, she knew, some were dazzled, but most others tended to respond to her quick intelligence and humour. Not Edward Merrick, apparently. It wasn't that he was openly rude or even ignoring her, but she couldn't shake the sense that he thought that she was a bit silly and superficial somehow.

Perdita couldn't put her finger on why she felt that. It might have been something to do with the arid edge to his voice when he spoke to her, or that disquieting gleam in the grey eyes that seemed to see much more than she really wanted them to. Whatever it was, Perdita didn't like it one little bit.

Naturally, she responded by ignoring him and sparkling even harder, and if that made Ed decide she was even sillier than he had thought, that was tough. *She* couldn't care less.

It didn't stop her keeping a surreptitious eye on him as she held court, but for once it felt like hard work. When she saw him leave at last, Perdita should have been able to relax and be herself, but instead the evening seemed suddenly flat.

It was time she rang her mother anyway. Laughingly refusing the offers of a last drink that were pressed on her, Perdita made her escape from the bar. It was a relief to stop smiling when she got outside and she frowned slightly as she walked along the long corridor to her room.

What was the matter with her? She wasn't usually like this. So Edward Merrick wasn't that taken with her? It didn't matter whether he liked her or not as long as they could have a good professional relationship. OK, that hadn't got off to the best of starts when she had called him pretentious, but she had apologised, and he hadn't seemed *that* bothered. There was no reason why they shouldn't work together perfectly well, and if Ed didn't want to be friends…well, she had plenty of friends already. She didn't care.

Much.

Throwing herself on her bed, Perdita pulled out her BlackBerry and pressed the short dial to call her mother.

'Mum? It's me,' she said when her mother answered. 'How are you?'

As always, Helen James insisted that she was absolutely fine, but Perdita couldn't help worrying about her. It was hard to put her finger on why, but her mother seemed to have got older and a little querulous quite suddenly. She wasn't as active as she had once been, and the house she had once kept so immaculately clean had begun to seem less well cared for, as if she couldn't be bothered with dusting and polishing any more.

Once or twice, Perdita had suggested getting her some help, but her mother refused point-blank to even consider the possibility. 'I'm not having strangers poking around in my private business!' she declared. 'I suppose you'll want to put me in a home next!'

She got so upset if Perdita tried to pursue the matter that, in the end, Perdita had to let it drop and took to calling in every couple of days instead to help out as discreetly as she could.

'Millie popped in to say hello,' her mother told her. 'She said she was just passing.'

Perdita was relieved to hear no hint of suspicion in Helen's voice. She had asked her best friend to look in on her mother while she was away on the course, but it had been a risk. If Helen had thought she was being checked up on, she would have been furious.

'Oh? How was she?'

'She's put on weight since her divorce,' her mother said disapprovingly. 'She'll have to be careful not to let herself go.'

Millie had more important things to worry about than her figure, Perdita reflected as she said goodbye to her mother.

Her husband had left her with a huge mortgage and the main responsibility for caring for two teenage daughters, and there had been times when her friend's buoyant sense of humour had been severely tested over the last few years.

Settling herself more comfortably against her pillows, Perdita rang Millie next to thank her. Typically, Millie brushed aside any gratitude. 'It was fun,' she said. 'I always liked your mum. I created an elaborate charade to explain why I was passing in case she decided to interrogate me— you know how scary she can be—but she didn't ask. I was quite disappointed!'

'How did you think she was?'

'She seemed fine to me,' said Millie. 'A bit older, of course, and I can see that she's difficult but, let's be honest, she was never the easiest of people in the first place, was she?'

'No, that's true.' Perdita sighed. She loved her mother, but she had always been a rather prickly character.

'Stop worrying about her and tell me about this course you're on instead.'

'It's ridiculous,' grumbled Perdita, obediently changing the subject. 'They've divided us into personality types and they keep telling me I'm a peacock!'

Millie hooted with laughter. 'I could have told them that!'

'You don't think I'd be a good dolphin?' asked Perdita, a little put out.

'Nope, you're definitely a peacock. Your new boss could have saved the company hundreds of pounds if he'd just asked me instead of forking out for a whole course.'

'Oh, talking of my new boss…he's here!' said Perdita, who had had enough of people failing to recognise the easy-going, fun-loving, dolphin aspects of her personality. She had thought Millie at least would have known her better!

'No!' Millie was gratifyingly intrigued by the news. 'What's he like?'

'Well, he's...' Perdita stopped, realising that she didn't really know how to describe Ed.

She knew what he *looked* like, could picture his face with alarming clarity, in fact: the cool eyes, the cool mouth, that unsettling gleam of humour. He had ordinary brown hair, greying at the temples, and that intriguing fan of laughter lines creasing the corner of his eyes. But she couldn't tell Millie *that*.

'He's not what I was expecting,' she finished lamely at last.

'Oh?' Millie prompted, drawing out the syllables with exaggerated effect. 'Attractive?'

'Not really... Well, sort of, I suppose...*I* don't know!' said Perdita, flustered when Millie started laughing.

'He sounds gorgeous!'

'He's not *gorgeous*,' snapped Perdita. 'He's just a *sensible* executive with greying hair who thinks I'm a bit silly.' She told Millie about her *faux pas* and Millie seemed to think that was funny too.

'It sounds as if you might have met your match at last, Perdita. Is he available?'

'He doesn't wear a wedding ring,' said Perdita, and then was furious with herself for admitting that she had noticed.

'Hmm...doesn't mean anything,' said Millie. 'Find out more tomorrow and report back to me!'

CHAPTER TWO

'THIS morning you'll all be divided into pairs and given a series of tasks to achieve.' Perdita slipped into the dining room as the chief facilitator was making his announcement at breakfast the next morning. Her morning routine always seemed to take twice as long in an unfamiliar bathroom and she was running late.

Grabbing a cup of coffee, she stood at the back and found herself scanning the room for Edward Merrick as she pretended to listen to the instructions for the day.

'You've all been allocated a task to complete at first on your own, but over the course of the day you should meet up with other pairs and eventually you'll form four large groups. It's important that you check the list in reception for the location of your first task before you go outside.'

Outside? Perdita grimaced. When she had pulled back her curtains that morning, she hadn't even been able to see the surrounding hills for the heavy grey cloud. Outside, the tree tops were swaying wildly in the wind, and rain streaked the big windows of the dining room.

She had been hoping that the facilitators would change their minds about running part of the course outside when they saw the conditions. Perdita was not a fan of the great outdoors and although wet weather gear had been specified in the joining instructions for the course she really didn't have anything suitable to wear. The jacket she had brought with her was adequate to protect her against a shower in the city but would be useless in this rain. She was going to get soaked, and it was all Ed Merrick's fault.

Perdita barely had time to swallow her coffee before everyone was filing out, apparently keen to start the day. They had all had the forethought to bring coats and boots downstairs but, of course, she had to run up to her room for hers. Really, it would be so much easier if they could just do all these stupid tasks indoors.

Wrapping a fuschia-pink pashmina around her throat for warmth, Perdita made her way reluctantly back down to find her partner. There was only person left in reception when she got there and, with a strange sense of inevitability, she saw that it was Edward Merrick.

'It looks as if we're meant to be together after all,' he greeted her.

Meant to be together… He was joking, that much was obvious, but the very idea made Perdita feel a bit odd.

'What's the reasoning behind pairing us off?' she asked, hoping that she sounded curious rather than as if her heart were pitter-pattering in the most absurd way at the prospect of being alone with him.

'I suspect it's because they think I'm the only one you might not be able to boss around,' he said, cocking a glance at the facilitator, who grinned as he nodded. 'We all saw how you couldn't help but take over every task you did yesterday. Today's a chance for the poor old dolphins and owls to develop their own leadership skills.'

'Oh, that's ridiculous!' said Perdita, exasperated, but

aware that a tiny part of her was pleased to be prodded out of her self-consciousness. 'I made a point of *not* taking over, in fact. I wasn't chairperson once.'

'No, but who decided that a chairperson was needed in the first place?' asked Ed. 'Who put forward a candidate every time and got everyone to agree?'

'Well…that's only because they were wasting time,' she said defensively. 'I just wanted the team to succeed. That's not the same as bossing everyone around!'

'Perhaps not, but you've got to admit that you're a hard woman to resist,' he said, and, although he didn't actually smile, the corners of his eyes creased and, as her gaze met his, Perdita felt her heart jerk alarmingly.

She pulled her pashmina tighter around her throat. 'You don't seem to have any problem resisting me,' she said crisply to disguise her sudden, embarrassing, breathlessness. 'Maybe I won't be able to resist *you*,' she added, and then wished that she hadn't. There were too many double meanings to all this talk of resistance and it unnerved her. 'Nobody seems to think *that* would be a problem, do they?'

Ed's gaze rested on her. The vividly coloured scarf was the perfect foil for her dark colouring. With her glossy hair, expressive face and those bright, dark eyes, she reminded him of a rather cross robin. At forty, she was far from the youngest woman on the course, and she was by no means the prettiest either, but there was a vivacity to her that made it hard to look at anyone else when she was there.

Perdita wasn't at all what he had been expecting. He had heard glowing reports of her efficiency, and her CV was undeniably impressive, but neither had done anything to prepare him for the reality of her. He had imagined an intensely professional, rather serious woman, dedicated to a career rather than to a family—and yes, maybe he *had* assumed that because he knew that she was single, Ed thought, rather ashamed of his own prejudices—but Perdita was nothing like that.

Nothing like that, in fact. She was sharp and funny instead of serious, extrovert rather than intense. Given her CV, it was obvious that she was perfectly capable of being professional, but Ed would never have guessed it from his covert observation of her so far. She evidently spent nearly as long grooming herself as his teenage daughter, which was saying something, and she was always perfectly made-up and stylishly dressed. All in all, she seemed far too frivolous for a forty-year-old operations manager.

And, while she might well be single and childless, as stated on her CV, he imagined there would be some man around. She was too attractive to be on her own, but even if she was, there was no sign whatsoever that she was unhappy with her lot. Indeed, she seemed to be having a better time than anyone else, judging by the laughter that surrounded her wherever she was. There was nothing wrong with enjoying yourself, Ed had found himself thinking irritably in the bar the previous night, but there was no need to do it quite so loudly. She was just a bit too…much.

Ed badly wanted to disapprove of Perdita, in fact, but was uneasily aware that he was intrigued by her too. He had more of a problem resisting her than Perdita knew, although he decided to keep that fact to himself.

'I think the idea is that we learn to work together without the need to resist each other at all,' he said in a carefully dry voice that earned him a sharp look from those dark eyes. Perdita might act as if she were silly and superficial sometimes, but she was no fool.

'What exactly is it that we have do?' she asked briskly, and Ed unfolded a map, relieved at the change of subject.

'We've got to get ourselves to here,' he said, pointing.

'And where are we now?' asked Perdita, peering at the map and wishing that she hadn't noticed what strong, capable-looking hands he had.

'Here.'

Her eyes followed one long, square-tipped finger. 'But that's miles!' she exclaimed, horrified.

'I don't think it'll be as bad as it looks, but we'd better get going.' Ed looked dubiously down at her feet. 'Are those the only boots you've got?'

'I didn't realise that the course involved trekking across the countryside in the pouring rain,' she said, regarding her boots mournfully. They were the most comfortable pair that she owned, but they were designed for city pavements, not windswept hillsides. 'They're going to be ruined.'

'They are,' Ed agreed without any noticeable sympathy. 'Didn't you read the instructions about bringing outdoor gear?'

Of course, he was practically dressed in a waterproof jacket, boots and wet weather trousers. Perdita eyed him with dislike. 'This *is* my outdoor gear,' she said. 'I don't do the outdoors.'

'You do now,' he said. 'Come on, let's go.'

Perdita pulled up the hood of her jacket as she followed him out through the doors.

'Ugh, it's horrible out here!' she said, reminding Ed forcibly of a cat, shaking its wet paws fastidiously. 'I don't know why I bothered to wash and dry my hair this morning,' she grumbled on. 'I'm going to get soaked!'

Pulling the zip of her jacket up as far as it would go, she screwed up her face against the rain. 'I really don't see why we can't do all this inside, like we did yesterday,' she went on. 'You know, if I was as dominating as you all make out, I would make them let us do just that. It's unfair of them to lull us into a false sense of security and then spring this on us today. They're just making us suffer for the sake of it!'

'Don't you think it's interesting to see how people react to different situations?'

'No, I *don't* think it's interesting,' she said, following him out of the hotel grounds and on to a tussocky hillside. 'I *might* think it were slightly more interesting if we were sitting inside, but even then I have my doubts. What I really think is that this whole course is a complete waste of time,' she added roundly. 'I just don't see how this is supposed to help me at work, to be frank. The only thing it's doing is making me wish that I was there rather than here. I could be warm and dry and catching up on all my work with a cup of coffee now.'

Ed shot her an amused glance as she trudged next to him 'Do you complain like this at work?'

'No, I like my job.'

'Even though you're over-qualified for it? I've read your CV,' he reminded her. 'It's very impressive. You used to work in London, and you spent a couple of years in New York and a stint in Paris.'

He could imagine her there, Ed thought. She had that sharp, sassy, city quality, and even in a waterproof jacket and quite unsuitable boots she managed to look chic.

'I'd have thought Ellsborough was a little slow for a woman like you,' he said, and she looked at him with that bright, challenging gaze.

'What do you mean by that?'

'Ellsborough is very attractive, and it's got lots going for it, but it's never going to have the buzz of a big city, is it? And you seem like someone who likes a buzz,' he tried to explain, thinking of how she had looked in the bar last night, the dark hair swinging glossily around her vivid face, that throaty laugh ringing out.

Perdita was someone who created a buzz all of her own, he realised wryly. Maybe she didn't need a big city.

Perdita wasn't quite sure how to take that. 'It's true, I like to have a good time,' she said. 'New York was fabulous, and I did love London. I would happily have stayed there for ever.'

'So what made you give it all up for Ellsborough?'

Digging her hands into her pockets, Perdita sighed. 'My father died two years ago and my mother was getting on… When a job came up at Bell Browning, it seemed sensible to apply so that I could go home before I had to. I was terrified that I might end up having to move back and not having anything to do. Ellsborough isn't exactly handy for commuting to London, and there aren't that many jobs there that fit my profile.'

And moving back to Ellsborough had seemed a good opportunity to leave Nick and all the sad memories of her time with him behind too, she remembered, although she didn't tell Ed that. His interest in her was purely professional. He wouldn't care about her broken heart.

'So you're a local girl?' he said.

She nodded. 'Yes. I couldn't wait to leave Ellsborough for the bright lights when I was growing up, I have to admit, but it's not so bad now. Bell Browning has been a good company to work for, and I can afford a much better standard of living in the north than I could in London. I've got a lovely flat and good friends…' Perdita trailed off, uneasily

aware that she sounded as if she were trying a little too hard
to convince herself that she was perfectly happy there.

'But you still miss the big city?'

'Sometimes.' Ed didn't say anything, but there was a disbelieving quality to his silence and she glanced at him from
under her hood. 'OK, more than sometimes,' she conceded.
'I do like what I do at Bell Browning, but yes, I miss the excitement of the City. It's not just the shops or the restaurants
or the fact that there's so much to do in London. It's a kind
of energy that you get day and night that you just don't get
in a small provincial city like Ellsborough.'

'So you don't regret your high-flying career?'

'Of course I do,' she said, 'but we don't always have a
choice, do we? We can't just walk away from our responsibilities, no matter how much we might wish that we could.'

Her mother had needed her, Nick hadn't wanted her. At
the time, it hadn't seemed to Perdita that she had much
option. Going back to Ellsborough had been the right
decision, yes, but that didn't mean she couldn't regret the
way things had turned out, did it?

Hearing the thread of bitterness in her voice, Ed studied
her profile with a new interest, seeing for the first time the
faint strain that underlay the surface sparkle. Perhaps her life
wasn't always as much fun as it seemed to a casual observer.
Ed knew all about responsibilities, knew all about putting
on a brave face for the world. Perhaps he would have to
revise his opinion of her, he thought. He, of all people,
should know that how things seemed on the surface weren't
always the way they really were.

Perdita had stopped for breath at the crest of a hummock
and was squinting into the rain. 'I can't see anything,' she
said. 'Are you sure we're going the right way?'

'I think so.' Ed stood near her to shelter the map from the rain and turned it round so that she could see. 'I reckon we're about here,' he said, pointing.

'Still miles to go, then.' Unsettled by his closeness, Perdita took what she hoped would be a casual step back, only to stumble over a tussock of grass. She would have fallen if Ed hadn't shot out a hand to catch her under the arm and haul her upright once more. His grip was hard and strong, and Perdita felt ridiculously breathless as he let her go.

'All right?'

'Yes…yes, I'm fine.' Her voice sounded all thin and silly. She just hoped he would put it down to her almost-fall.

'Do you want a rest?'

She shook her head. The sooner they found some other people, the better. 'We'll just get wetter and colder if we stop. Let's go on.'

They set off in a diagonal line across and down the hillside, heading for the river that was hidden in the murky mist at the bottom of the valley—at least according to Ed's map. Perdita was very conscious of him walking beside her. He never slipped or tripped the way she kept doing, but moved with an easy, deliberate stride.

Of course, that would be the panther in him, Perdita tried to joke herself out of this disturbing awareness of him, but it didn't really work. Even in this dreary light, he seemed extraordinarily well-defined, with a solidity and a steadiness that was both reassuring and unsettling at the same time. With her head bent against the rain, she couldn't see much of his face, but if she peeked under her hood she could catch a glimpse of the edge of his mouth and, in spite of her cold feet and the rain trickling inside her collar, something warm would flicker and glow deep within her.

Any extra warmth should have been welcome in this weather but, frankly, it was making Perdita decidedly edgy. A decent jacket, gloves, thick socks…that was the kind of warmth she needed, not this melting, squirmy feeling she got whenever she looked at a man who was not only her boss, but was also responsible for her being out here in the first place.

Huddling herself deeper into her coat, she plodded on and did her best to ignore him, or at least ignore the way he was making her feel, but when Ed broke the silence by asking her what she did with herself when she wasn't at work, she snapped at him.

'What's with the interrogation?' she asked sharply, and Ed raised his brows at her tone.

'I just thought this would be a good opportunity to learn a bit more about each other,' he said, lifting his hands in a gesture of conciliation.

'I'm not learning much about you, I notice!'

'What do you want to know?'

A little flustered by the open invitation to ask him about himself, Perdita hesitated.

Of course what she *really* wanted to know was whether he was married, or if had a girlfriend, but she could hardly ask that, could she? Not when he had read her CV and presumably knew that she was single.

'Why are you moving to Ellsborough?' she asked instead, mentally shushing Millie, who would be furious to know that she had passed up such a golden opportunity to ask about his personal life. 'You thought it was odd that I'd ended up there, but I wasn't nearly such a high-flyer as you,' she pointed out. 'We've all heard about the companies you've run in London, and Bell Browning is a very small fish compared to them.' She sent him one of her sharp glances. 'You're not planning to carve it up and sell it on, are you?'

'No,' said Ed. 'It's a sound company. There's plenty to do, of course, but I see no reason to restructure—not yet, anyway.'

Perdita was only partially reassured. 'Still, it's not much of challenge for a man who's been chief executive of some household names the way you have.'

'I don't know. It could be quite a challenge dealing with my new staff if you're anything to go by,' he said, but his smile glinted and Perdita despised herself for the way that treacherous warmth in the pit of her stomach spread insidiously through her veins at the sight of it.

'Won't you miss London, though?' she asked, mentally dousing herself inside.

'To be honest, I haven't had time to appreciate living in London for a while now,' said Ed with a sigh. 'I wanted to downsize and move somewhere new, somewhere less frenetic, so when the opportunity at Bell Browning came up, I took it. A small, specialist company targeting niche markets will be an interesting change, and I'm looking forward to it, but it's not really about me. The whole family needs a fresh start.'

So he had a family. Damn.

Come on, Perdita caught herself up, alarmed by the depth of her disappointment. *What were you thinking? How many attractive men in their forties do you know who don't have a wife and kids? Of course he was always going to have a family!*

'Oh?' was the best she could manage as a response.

'My wife died five years ago,' Ed told her as they scrambled down a steep path, and Perdita was immediately overwhelmed by guilt for having been disappointed, even briefly, at the thought that he was 'taken'.

'Since then, I've been trying to keep the kids on an even

keel,' he went on. 'At first it seemed better to keep them in a familiar environment, but…well, the fact is that my son has been in trouble recently,' he admitted. 'He's not a bad boy, but he got in with the wrong crowd.'

He caught himself up with a twisted smile. 'I'm sure every parent says that,' he acknowledged, 'but Tom really *is* OK.'

'I'm sure he is,' said Perdita quickly. 'I'm so sorry to hear about your wife, Ed,' she added, picking her words with care. 'I didn't realise that you were a widower. It must be very difficult bringing up children on your own.'

'Especially when they start going off the rails,' he said ruefully. 'Tom's always been quite withdrawn—he's much less resilient than the girls—which is why I didn't really know how to cope when things went wrong. I'm hoping the move will give him a fresh start, though. He's due to start at sixth-form college in September, so the idea is that we'll move to Ellsborough at the end of the summer and they can all begin a new term at their new schools.'

'All?' Perdita wasn't sure *how* she felt now. She had gone from an uneasy attraction to disappointment at hearing that he had a family and then guilt at discovering his personal tragedy. The sensible thing would be to feel absolutely nothing for him at all, but that didn't seem to be an option at the moment. Best to stick to polite interest, she decided, and put her feelings away to be examined later when she was on her own. 'How many children have you got?'

'Three,' said Ed. 'Tom's the eldest, and then there's Cassie, who's fifteen going on twenty-five, and Lauren is just fourteen.'

Perdita wondered how two teenage girls who were used to the big city would get on in provincial Ellsborough. It had been hard enough for her, and she had been coming back to a place she already knew. 'How do they feel about leaving London?' she asked carefully.

'They're complaining like mad, of course,' said Ed, 'but they're much more sociable and confident than their brother. I think they'll cope OK—I hope so, anyway, as it's too late now. I've bought a house and we exchanged contracts yesterday, so if all goes well we'll be able to move at the beginning of September.'

'Where is it?'

'Not far from the centre. It's an area called Flaxton—do you know it?'

Perdita nodded. 'It's the other side of town from me,' she said. 'My mother lives there, in fact.' Flaxton was a part of the town known for its big, comfortable Edwardian houses, but she would have expected Ed to have chosen somewhere a little more exclusive. He must have earned a packet in London. 'I'm surprised you didn't go for one of the villages around Ellsborough, though. Some of them are lovely.'

'It's too easy to spend all evening as a taxi service when you've got three teenagers in the house,' said Ed wryly. 'They want to be out with their friends, not stuck in the country with me. And since I'm making them move away from London, buying a house near the centre is a compromise I can make.'

He was putting his kids first, the way Nick had always done, thought Perdita, and that was how it should be. Still, she couldn't help feeling depressed as they trudged the rest of the way to the river.

Not that she had any business feeling depressed. It wasn't as if there had ever been any prospect of a relationship, anyway. Ed hadn't given the slightest indication that he was ever likely to see her as more than a colleague. But if he *had*,

Perdita tried to reason with herself, it would have been depressing to realise that it would never have worked.

She had already had a relationship with a single father, and it had been too hard. She wasn't going to put herself in the position of always being second-best again, so it would never have been a runner with Ed, anyway, she told herself firmly.

Oh, and a relationship with your boss was never a good idea either, she remembered a little belatedly. No, Edward Merrick was definitely out of bounds for all sorts of good reasons.

The fact that he had a mouth that made her weak at the knees was neither here nor there.

'It wasn't as if he was *that* attractive,' she told Millie when she got home the following day and had endured an interrogation about Edward Merrick and his entire emotional history.

Millie wasn't convinced. 'It sounds a sinful waste to me,' she said. 'The poor man's been a widower for five years. This move will be a fresh start for him too, remember. I bet you anything he gets snapped up as soon as he arrives—and if you hold his children against him, you'll miss your chance and you'll only have yourself to blame!'

'I don't want a chance,' said Perdita loftily. 'All I'm looking for with Ed Merrick is a good professional relationship.'

And, given that she had started off by insulting him, followed up by grumbling about the course he'd sent her on and showing off in the bar every night, she might have to work quite hard just to have that.

Not that she had the chance to build any kind of relationship with him for some time. The dreary June turned into a changeable July and a belated burst of summer in August, but Edward Merrick made only fleeting visits to Bell Browning in that time. Perdita saw him once, getting into a lift with fellow directors, and another time walking across the car park, deep in conversation with the head of human resources, but she wasn't invited to meet him.

It wasn't that she wanted to see him again particularly, but she couldn't help feeling a little miffed. Didn't he think the Operations department important? And, come to think of it, weren't they supposed to have bonded on that stupid course?

Luckily, she was too busy to spend too much time thinking about him. There was plenty to keep her occupied at work, and her mother caught a chill at the end of July which left her frailer and more irascible than normal. Perdita thought she was vaguer, too, although her will was as strong as ever. She was still stubbornly resistant to the idea that she might have any kind of outside help, and Perdita took to going over every evening to make sure her mother had something to eat and to tidy up as much as she could.

So it was only very occasionally that she remembered Edward Merrick. When she did, it was always with a sense of shock that she could picture him so vividly: the grey eyes, the stern mouth, that elusive glinting smile. It was odd when she hardly thought about him at all.

Well, not much anyway.

One cool evening in early September, Perdita pulled into the drive of the rambling Edwardian house where she had grown up, and where her mother still lived. A huge removal van was backed into the next door drive, she noticed with relief. It looked as if someone was moving in at last. The house had been on the market for ages and she hadn't liked her mother living with an empty house on one side. She needed all the understanding neighbours she could get.

It looked as if the removal men were almost finished. Perdita switched off the engine and sat in the car for a minute. It was something she often did nowadays. She knew she was just putting off the moment when she had to get out of the car and go inside, but it gave her a chance to steel herself for any changes in her mother.

Sometimes there were just tiny indications that she was losing control. Perdita got her fastidiousness from her mother, and seeing her with a stain on her shirt or an unwashed pile of dishes in the sink was heartbreaking confirmation that, however much she resisted it, her mother was declining. Occasionally, though, her mother would be brighter and so much her old self that Perdita let herself hope that she might be getting better after all.

'I hate you!'

Perdita was startled out of her thoughts by the sight of a very pretty teenage girl flouncing out of the neighbouring house. 'I wish we'd never come here! I'm going back to London!' she shouted at someone inside and, slamming the front door, she stormed past the removal men, who were rolling up cloths and carrying empty packing cases back into the van, and stalked off down the road.

Suppressing a smile, Perdita got out of the car at last. She remembered stomping off down that very same road on a regular basis when she was a teenager. Her mother had never bothered chasing after her either.

The memory of her mother as she had been then made her smile fade as she let herself into the house. 'Mum, it's me!'

She found her mother in the kitchen, peering uneasily through the window at the house next door. 'There's new people next door,' she said, sounding fretful. 'I hope they won't be noisy.'

Perdita thought of the slammed front door. 'I'm sure they won't,' she said soothingly. 'You won't hear them anyway.'

Picking up a can from the counter, she sniffed at it cautiously and wrinkled her nose at the smell. 'Why don't I make some supper?' she said brightly, trying to distract her mother from the window as she poured the contents away down the sink and rinsed out the can. 'I've brought some chicken. I thought I could grill it the way you like.'

'Oh, it's all right, dear. I've made supper.'

'Oh?' Perdita looked around with a sinking heart. Helen James had once been a wonderful cook, but her recent attempts had been very erratic.

'A casserole. It's in the oven.'

But when Perdita looked in the oven it was stone cold. She took out the uncooked stew and wanted to weep. 'I think you must have forgotten to turn it on,' she said as cheerfully as she could. 'It'll take too long to cook now. I'll do the chicken instead.'

All through supper her mother fretted about the fact that there were new people next door. She worried about the noise and whether the children would run into the garden, repeating herself endlessly until Perdita had to grit her teeth to stop herself snapping. Eventually she suggested that she went and introduced herself to the new neighbours.

'I'll tell them that you don't want them in the garden,' she said, reflecting that it might not be a bad idea to go round and make contact in any case. She would be able to leave her phone numbers in case there was ever a problem.

'Oh, would you, dear?'

'I'll take them a bottle of wine as a housewarming present.'

Settling her mother in front of the television after supper, Perdita cleared up the kitchen and then went down to the cellar where her father's store was still kept. He had loved his wine and it always made Perdita feel sad to see how many bottles he had never had the chance to enjoy.

She selected a bottle, blew the dust off and headed next door. August's brief burst of heat seemed to have disappeared as suddenly as it had arrived and a light drizzle was falling, settling on Perdita like a gossamer web as she crossed the drive.

Reaching the front door, Perdita hesitated before ringing the bell. Should she be doing this? The poor people were probably exhausted after their move and the last thing they would want was a neighbour turning up. On the other hand, the idea that she would make contact appeared to have soothed her mother. She didn't really want to go back and say that she hadn't done it. She wouldn't stay long, though. She would simply hand over the bottle and explain who she was.

There was such a long silence after she rang that Perdita was about to turn and leave when, with a clatter of shoes on a tiled hall floor, the door was abruptly opened by the same girl she had last seen striding furiously down the road. Perdita thought it tactful not to ask if she had decided better of returning to London.

'Hello,' she said instead with a smile. 'I'm sorry to disturb you, but I've just come from next door. I've brought this,' she said, holding up the bottle. 'Just to welcome you to the street and ask if there's anything I can do for you.'

'Can you get Dad to take us back to London?' the girl asked, taking her literally, and Perdita suppressed a smile. Here was someone who wasn't at all happy about being in Ellsborough, obviously.

'I was thinking more about lending a cup of sugar, that kind of thing.'

'Oh. OK.' The girl sighed, then turned and bellowed up

the staircase in a voice that belied her slight frame. 'Dad! It's the neighbour!'

There was a pause, followed by a muffled shout of, 'Coming!' A few moments later, Perdita heard the sound of feet echoing on the uncarpeted staircase and she turned, a welcoming smile pinned to her face, only for it to freeze in shock as she saw who had reached the bottom of the stairs.

Ed Merrick.

CHAPTER THREE

PERDITA's heart lurched into her throat. The sight of him was a physical shock, a charge of recognition that surged and crackled through her body so powerfully that she felt jarred and jolted. She barely knew the man, after all. He shouldn't seem so startlingly familiar. Ed was looking tired and more than a little grubby in a T-shirt and jeans but the keen eyes were just the same as she had remembered. He had the same mouth, the same air of cool competence, the same ability to discompose her just by standing there.

'It's you,' she said stupidly.

Ed looked equally surprised to see her, and for one awful moment she thought that she was going to have to remind him who she was, but then his face cleared and he was coming towards her with a smile.

'Perdita…' For once Ed seemed to have lost his normal composure. 'Sorry…you're the last person I was expecting…'

Ed, in fact, was completely thrown by the sight of Perdita standing in his hall, as slender and as vivid as ever, throwing her surroundings into relief and yet making them seem faintly drab in comparison.

He remembered her so clearly from the course in June, and had been looking forward to seeing her again. He had hoped to bump into her on one of his visits to Bell Browning over the summer, but he hadn't had so much as a glimpse of her. He had asked, very casually, if she were around one day, but she had been away then for some reason and he hadn't wanted to push it by asking again.

There would be time to get to know her when he moved permanently, Ed reasoned. People would think that he was interested in her, which he wasn't, or at least, not in that way. Quite apart from the fact that he was pretty sure someone like her would already be in a relationship, she wasn't at all his type. It wasn't that he couldn't see that she was attractive, in a striking rather than a pretty way, but she was nothing like Sue, for instance, who had been soft and sweet and calm and loving. There was nothing soft or sweet about Perdita. She was edgy and astringent and restless and when she was around, calm was the last thing Ed felt.

Her performance on the last day of that course had exasperated and impressed him in equal measure. In spite of all her complaints and in spite of the rain, she had contributed more than anyone else to the success of the tasks, and Ed was fairly sure that she had enjoyed herself too. Her ability to motivate and defuse tension with humour was extraordinary, he had thought. So he had remembered her, yes, but only because she was such an impossible person to forget. He wasn't *interested*.

So he was rather taken aback by the way every sense in his body seemed to leap with pleasure at the sight of her.

Perdita herself seemed less than delighted to see him, and he stopped himself before he found himself greeting her with quite inappropriate warmth.

There was an awkward pause. 'What on earth are you doing here?' Ed asked after a moment.

It sounded all too much like an accusation to Perdita, who flushed. 'I…my mother lives next door,' she said, ridiculously flustered by the situation. 'We saw the removal vans so guessed you'd just moved in. I just popped over to welcome you and give you this.' She held up the bottle of wine awkwardly.

'That's very kind,' said Ed as he wiped his hands on his jeans. 'Sorry, I'm filthy,' he explained and took the bottle Perdita was holding out to him. His brows shot up as he read the label. 'This is more than just a bottle of wine! I hope you're going to stay and share it with me?'

'Oh, no, I mustn't,' Perdita stammered, stepping back, as gauche as a schoolgirl. 'You must be tired if you've been moving all day.'

'Please,' said Ed, and unfairly he smiled. 'I've had a long day and you don't know how much I've been wishing that I could just sit down with a glass of wine! I can't share it with the kids, and I don't like to drink alone.'

'Well…' Now it would seem ungracious if she rushed off, Perdita decided. 'I mustn't stay long, though. I've left my mother on her own.'

'Have a glass anyway. Everything's chaos, but come into the kitchen and I'll see if I can lay my hands on a corkscrew.'

Ed's daughter looked from one to the other suspiciously. 'Do you guys know each other, then?'

'Your father is my boss,' Perdita told her.

'And this is my daughter, Cassie, as you've probably gathered,' Ed put in.

Cassie tossed her blonde hair over her shoulder. 'God, is he as grumpy at work as he is at home?'

'You'd probably need to ask his PA,' said Perdita, amused. 'I haven't had much to do with him yet.'

'It's no use asking his PAs. They always think he's lovely, but we know better,' said Cassie with a dark look at her father. 'At home, he's a tyrant! He's so pig-headed and unreasonable!'

'Really?'

'I couldn't bear to work for him,' Cassie declared. 'I'd be on strike the whole time!'

Ed seemed quite unfazed by all of this as he led the way into the big kitchen at the back of the house. 'I'm so unreasonable that after a day moving house with three bone-idle teenagers, I decided that it was more important to sort out some beds so that we could all sleep tonight, rather than dropping everything to set up the computer so that Cassie could instant message her friends right away.'

'Very tyrannical,' murmured Perdita.

'See?' Cassie shook back her hair and changed tack without warning. 'Can I have some wine?'

'No,' said Ed.

Cassie heaved a dramatic sigh. 'I'm going to go and ring India and tell her how *boring* it is here!' she announced and, when this threat had no visible effect on her father, she flounced out.

'Sorry about that,' said Ed, locating the corkscrew at last in one of the boxes piled on the kitchen counters. 'Cassie is a bit of a drama queen, as you probably gathered.'

'She's very pretty.'

'And knows it,' he said wryly. 'When Cassie is in a good mood, there's no one more delightful—and no one more unpleasant when she's in a temper! It can be exhausting just keeping up with her moods.'

'My best friend has two teenage girls,' said Perdita, who had spent many hours plying Millie with wine and listening to the latest crisis with either Roz or Emily, and occasionally both. 'I gather they can be hard work. It always seems that boys are easier, but that's probably because Millie doesn't have one!'

Ed smiled ruefully. 'Probably. Tom can be just as difficult in his own way, and so can Lauren. They're upstairs, but I'll spare you the introductions for now. It's been a long day and for now I'd just like to sit down and relax for a few minutes!'

He pulled out a chair from the kitchen table. 'Are you OK here? The sitting room is even more of a mess, I'm afraid.'

'Here's fine.' Perdita watched as Ed poured the wine and then burrowed his nose in the glass reverently. Something about the intentness of his expression, something about his smile, something about the hand curving around the glass made her squirm inside and she wriggled involuntarily in her chair.

Ed lifted his head and smiled at her across the table. 'This is a wonderful wine. Do you always give away bottles like this to your neighbours?'

'No, it was just the first one I found in my father's collection,' she told him. 'I don't know anything about wine, to be honest. I'm sure Dad would be glad to know it had gone to someone who appreciates it, though.'

'I remember you said your father had died.' Ed took another appreciative sip and put his wine down. 'Does your mother live on her own?'

'For the moment.' Perdita turned her own glass very carefully by the stem. 'That's one of the reasons I came round, actually. I wanted to give her new neighbours my contact numbers in case there was ever any problem. She hasn't been well recently, and it's taking her a long time to get over it. I try to come every day, but she's alone at night and when I'm at work, and that does worry me sometimes. Some days she seems fine, but others she's not so good.'

'Couldn't you get someone to come in and help her?' said Ed. 'When my own mother was ill, she had excellent carers. There was someone in the house with her twenty-four hours a day.'

'I've tried suggesting that, but she won't hear of it.' Perdita sighed and stopped fiddling with her glass, taking a sip of wine instead. 'Sometimes I think that the only thing keeping her going is her determination not to lose her privacy. That's really important to people of her generation. I do understand. It must be awful to feel dependent, but it's so frustrating too. Her life—and mine!—would be so much easier if she would let someone pop in and cook and clean at least. As it is—'

She broke off, embarrassed suddenly. Too often lately she had found herself going on and on about her mother's situation, as if it consumed her. It wasn't a healthy sign.

'As it is,' Ed finished for her in a practical voice, 'you have to do everything. Isn't there anyone else in the family who could help, or are you an only child?'

'No, I've got two brothers, but one emigrated to New Zealand a couple of years ago, and the other lives in Devon and is married with three small children, so obviously he can't be expected to help, especially when there's me with no husband or family to take into account. It goes without saying that *I* have to be the one to give up my life.'

She broke off abruptly. 'Sorry, I should have a paper bag to put over my head when I start going on like this!' she apologised. 'It's just that I get so resentful sometimes, and then I feel guilty. The fact is that I don't want to give up my job to look after my mother. I don't know how I would

manage financially, but perhaps that's just an excuse? My
mother spent enough years of her life looking after me, after
all. Am I just being selfish in not selling my flat and moving
in as a full-time carer?'

'I don't think so.' Ed frowned as he considered her situation. He could quite see how frustrating she found it. 'It does
seem hard that all the responsibility falls on you. Couldn't
your brothers at least help persuade your mother that she
needs some practical care?'

'Mum doesn't believe in worrying men about domestic
details,' she said wryly. 'She's always so thrilled to hear
from them that, of course, she tells them everything is fine—
and then tells me at length how good it was of them to have
called her when they have such busy lives!'

Hearing the bitterness in her voice, she flushed. Ed was
a sympathetic listener. Too sympathetic, perhaps. He didn't
gush, or exclaim, or tell her how awful it was for her. He just
sat there and listened with a thoughtful expression that made
her want to blurt out all the worry and grief and frustration
and resentment bottled up inside.

But he had problems enough of his own and, anyway, he
was her boss. Remember that, Perdita?

'I'm sorry,' she said wearily. 'I shouldn't be like this. I
love my mother. I should be grateful that I've still got her,
not moaning about what a worry she is.'

'It's normal to feel resentment,' said Ed. 'When you love
someone, it's hard to cope with the fact that they can't be
what you need them to be any more. I loved Sue very much,'
he told Perdita, 'and I miss her still, but there were times
when I was angry with her for getting ill, for dying, for
leaving me to cope on my own, for leaving the kids without
a mother…I had to try and be strong for her and for the kids,

and yes, I resented the fact that there seemed to be no one to help me be strong.'

His mouth twisted. 'I hated myself for how I felt,' he said honestly. 'And I felt guilty about it, the way you do. If I'd been able to stand back and analyse the situation dispassionately, I'd have been less hard on myself. I'd have been able to see that anger can sometimes be a mechanism for dealing with fear.'

'Did your wife know how you felt?'

'I think so. I tried so hard not to take it out on her, but she knew me very well. And, of course, she was afraid too. Things were better when we both just admitted it, and then we could help each other.'

Perdita swallowed. 'I feel terrible going on about my mother when you've been through so much worse,' she confessed, but Ed shook his head.

'It's not a matter of "worse" or "better". You can't compare how it feels to lose someone you love. You can't say it's better to lose a partner through death rather than through divorce, or that it's easier to lose someone in spirit than physically, that you don't grieve as much for a mother as for a wife... However it happens,' he said, 'you have to deal with the pain of not having the person you love any more.'

'Still...' said Perdita, not entirely convinced. She thought Ed was probably just trying to make her feel better. 'How did you manage?' she asked tentatively after a moment.

'After Sue died?'

'Yes. It must have been so...' Perdita struggled to find the right word to express how she imagined he'd felt, but 'terrible', 'awful', 'sad' just sounded like trite clichés. 'So lonely,' she said after a pause. 'So desolate.'

Desolate was a good word, Ed thought. 'Yes, it was a

terrible time,' he said slowly, remembering Sue's hand, so painfully thin in his, the deafening, unbelievable silence when she'd stopped breathing at last. The expression in Tom's eyes when he'd told him that his mother was dead. Holding Lauren and feeling how her small body was racked by sobs. The fury in Cassie's face. She hadn't really believed until then that her mother would actually leave her. The tearing grief that had clawed at him when he'd tried to imagine the utter emptiness of a future without Sue by his side.

Ed shook the painful memories aside. 'For a while, you just have to go through the motions,' he told Perdita. 'Nothing seems to make any sense. But I couldn't fall apart. I had to keep the kids going somehow, and it wasn't easy.'

'They were terribly young to lose their mother,' said Perdita quietly.

'Lauren was only eight.'

Eight. She was forty, and the thought of losing her own mother filled her with dread. Perdita felt very ashamed of the fuss she had been making about caring for her mother earlier.

'There were practical problems to be dealt with too,' Ed was saying. 'My sister came for a while when Sue was dying, but she has her own life and she couldn't stay for ever. I wanted to find a nice, comfortable housekeeper, but they're not easy to come by and the kids wouldn't accept anyone else living in the house for a while—a bit like your mother, in fact! So we moved to a place where there was a flat over the garage where an au pair could live. None of them were very successful, though. It was really just someone to be in the house when the kids got home from school, but once Lauren got to secondary school, they said they didn't want anyone any more.

'They're used to getting themselves around London, but

it's one of the reasons I wanted to move to a smaller place, where I'm hoping they'll make a network of friends who live nearby instead of the other side of London. And somewhere I can get home more easily, and have a less pressurised job. Although they're all old enough to look after themselves in lots of ways, in others they need just as much attention now as when they were toddlers.'

He looked around the kitchen. 'So here we are! I'm hoping I've done the right thing, but it's always difficult to be certain. The girls are moaning about having to leave their friends in London and everything's a mess… It'll take us all a little time to settle down, I think.'

'And the last thing you need is me burdening you with my problems,' said Perdita guiltily. 'It sounds as if you've got more than enough of your own.'

'That doesn't make yours any less important,' said Ed, thinking how surprisingly easy it was to talk to Perdita. He didn't usually tell virtual strangers about Sue. She had been so effervescent and lively on the course that he would never have been able to imagine talking to her like this then, but she seemed oddly right sitting at his kitchen table now. She was no less vivid but her dark brown eyes were warm and sympathetic, and looking into them Ed felt the tight feeling in his chest loosen for the first time in years.

He made himself look away. 'My own mother died a couple of years ago, so I know what it's like,' he said gruffly.

A silence fell. It wasn't that uncomfortable at first but, as it lengthened, it began to tighten and tighten until it seemed to stretch and twang and, the longer it went on, the more impossible it seemed to break it.

Perdita was drinking her wine with a kind of desperation. Her father would have been appalled to know that she might as well have been drinking pop for all she could taste. She was too aware of Ed across the table from her, of the planes of his face, the angle of his jaw, the line of his mouth… Her blood thrummed and her mouth was so dry, she had to moisten her lips. Was it just her, or was there a dangerous charge in the atmosphere?

She made herself look around the kitchen as if fascinated by its design, but her gaze kept drifting back to Ed and, every time it did, their eyes would catch and snare and the air evaporated from the room, leaving her with a rushing in her ears and a scary sensation pulsing beneath her skin.

Perdita fought to get a grip. This wouldn't do. This was Edward Merrick. Her *boss*, remember?

'More wine?' he said, lifting the bottle, and his voice seemed to jar in the silence.

'No…thanks…' For heaven's sake! She was blushing and stammering as she drained her glass, squirming with embarrassment in case Ed somehow guessed the physical attraction—oh, why be mealy mouthed? Perdita asked herself impatiently—the sheer *lust* that had her in its grip. 'I should probably be getting back,' she said, horrified to hear the words come out as a croak.

'Are you sure?'

'Yes.' Pushing back her chair, she got abruptly to her feet. 'My mother will be expecting me.'

It wasn't true, but Ed wasn't to know that and Perdita was suddenly desperate to get away before she made a complete fool of herself. Perhaps she could blame it on the wine, she thought wildly. If it were as good as Ed said, there was no knowing what effect it might be having.

Ed escorted her to the door. 'Did you want to leave those numbers?'

'Numbers?'

'In case we need to get hold of you about your mother,' he prompted. 'I've got your work number, of course, but presumably your mobile would be better.'

'Oh…yes…of course.' Feeling foolish, Perdita dug in her pocket for the business card she had brought with her. 'I've written my personal numbers on the back.'

He took it from her. Was it her imagination, or was he being just as careful as she was to make sure that their fingers didn't touch? 'I'll put it up in kitchen and make sure the kids know about it.'

'Thanks.' There was a pause. Empty-handed now, Perdita lifted her arms from her sides and then let them drop again uselessly. 'Well…thanks.'

'Thank *you* for the wine.'

Another moment of awkwardness, then Ed forced a smile. 'I'll see you at work, then,' he said, horribly conscious of the constraint in the atmosphere. 'I've got tomorrow and the weekend to sort things out here, then I'm starting full-time on Monday.'

Work. Yes, remember that, Perdita told herself sternly. That place where he was Chief Executive and she was Operations Manager and there was no time for mooning around over grieving widowers with three children to look after.

'Of course,' she said brightly.

'We'll need to set up a meeting then.'

'Right,' she said. This was terrible. It was obvious that he couldn't wait for her to go any more than she could wait to be gone, but somehow neither of them seemed to be able to make it happen. 'Well, I'd better go,' she said, turning determinedly for the door. 'Bye.'

Her dignified exit was spoiled when she tripped over the

step as she left, but by then Perdita was feeling so awkward she was beyond embarrassment. Maybe it *was* the wine, she thought as she made her way back to her mother's house on legs that didn't seem to be working properly.

Definitely the wine, Perdita decided that weekend. By Monday she had herself well under control and had put the entire silly incident down to a mixture of tiredness and Cabernet Sauvignon, and if she had the odd, shameful *frisson* whenever she thought about seeing Ed again, she put it down to erratic air-conditioning.

A meeting of all the staff was called for the Monday afternoon so that Ed could address the entire company. He was an engaging speaker, and it was clear that he had made a good impression on everyone from the board members to the cleaners who were included in the meeting. Only Perdita left feeling distinctly aggrieved.

She had assumed that when Ed had talked about setting up a meeting he had meant on Monday, but she had just been part of a crowd, never a feeling that she liked. Perhaps he would try and see her on Tuesday?

But Tuesday came and went, as did Wednesday, and Perdita began to get cross. Didn't he care about Operations?

In the end, it was Friday before Perdita's secretary came into her office, bursting with news, and told her that Ed wanted to see her as soon as convenient. 'Shall I tell his PA you can go now?'

'No!' said Perdita instinctively, with just a hint of panic. Having sulked because he didn't appear to want to see her, she was abruptly flustered at the prospect.

Typical! She had dressed so carefully the last four days in the expectation that she would have a meeting with him, and now, just when she had given up expecting the summons, he had sprung it on her the day she was wearing her old-fashioned hound's-tooth suit instead of her fabulous cherry-pink jacket with the shawl collar and the flattering cut. She had been so determined to make a good impression.

For professional reasons, of course.

'You haven't got any meetings until twelve o'clock,' Valerie pointed out.

'Well, no…but I want to get this budget done first,' said Perdita, with a very fair assumption of casualness.

Why should she jump up and run along to his office the moment Ed snapped his fingers, after all? He had waited this long to see her. Let him wait a bit longer. The last thing she wanted was to look too keen. 'Ask his PA if she can fit me in some time this afternoon.'

It was all very well not wanting to appear keen, but Perdita hadn't reckoned with the fact that she would then waste the rest of morning feeling ridiculously nervous at the prospect of seeing Ed again. She did her best to concentrate on her budget—and it *did* need to be done—but the columns of figures kept wavering in front of her eyes and she would find her mind drifting back to his kitchen and how it had felt to sit opposite him, how he had smiled, how the air had leaked out of her lungs whenever she looked into his eyes or thought about his mouth.

And now she was going to see him again. Perdita's heart slowed to an uncomfortable thud, which was stupid. She was forty, much too old to be getting into a tizzy about a man. This wasn't some date. She was meeting her boss this afternoon, that was all. Anyone would think that she was excited, which clearly she wasn't.

One, because she didn't believe in mixing personal and

professional relationships, and this one was clearly only ever going to be professional anyway.

Two, because he had three children and she was never, ever going to get involved with a single father again.

And three, because she wasn't particularly attracted to him anyway. He was just a not particularly good-looking, middle-aged man, as she had told Millie. He wasn't even her type. That strange surge of desire she had felt the other evening was down to the wine and nothing else.

Still, she found herself in the Ladies just before the meeting Valerie had arranged for two o'clock, carefully applying a fresh coat of lipstick. When she had finished, Perdita inspected her reflection carefully. With her dark eyes, bold mouth and hair that swung in a glossy bob to her jaw line, she could take bright colours and dramatic outfits, but this suit was a classic. It had a pencil skirt and a chic jacket over a neat silky top, and Perdita decided on balance that it was probably a better look than the pink jacket currently languishing in the dry cleaners. This outfit might not be as striking, but it made her look cool, businesslike and thoroughly professional.

And not as if her heart were fluttering in her throat, which was all that mattered.

Perdita picked up her file, gave her jacket a final tug into place, took a deep breath and headed along to the Chief Executive's office.

Ed got to his feet when she went in and at the sight of him the breath promptly whooshed out of Perdita's lungs, just as it had done when he had appeared at the bottom of the stairs in his hallway. Today, he was wearing a shirt and tie and the formal wear made him seem older and more distant than the work-stained T-shirt and faded jeans.

Perdita was conscious of a rush of quite unfamiliar shyness. At least she thought it was shyness. Whatever it was, it left her with rubbery bones and a strange, quivering feeling beneath her skin.

Ridiculous.

She was Operations Manager of a successful company, Perdita reminded herself sternly. She was an intelligent, confident, capable forty-year-old woman, and she did *not* do shy or fluttery.

Tilting her chin, she smiled brightly and disguised her weird reaction with a show of briskness. She might feel strange, but she had no intention of letting Ed Merrick guess that it was related to him in any way.

'Thanks for taking the time to see me,' she said coolly as he waved her to the comfortable chairs in the corner of his office.

'Not at all,' said Ed. 'I'm glad you could fit me in.' Was there just the slightest suspicion of sarcasm in his voice? Perdita wondered suspiciously and she fought down a faint flush.

'It's a busy time in Operations.'

'So I gather,' Ed agreed smoothly. 'That's why I left you to last. I've seen all the other managers, but I knew that you could be counted on to carry on doing a good job without any interference from me.'

'Oh.' Perdita realised that she was sitting nervously on the edge of her chair and tried to relax. Leaning back a little, she crossed her legs, but that made her skirt ride up, exposing rather too much of her legs, so she uncrossed them again. She wished she was wearing trousers, as she would have done with her pink jacket.

Now what was she going to with her legs? Perhaps she could try crossing her ankles like royalty? But when she tried it, that felt all wrong too.

If Ed was irritated by her fidgeting, he didn't show it. 'Thank you again for the wine you brought the other day,' he said formally. 'It was a very nice thought.'

'You're welcome,' said Perdita with a rather off-putting brightness. 'It's easy to be generous with someone else's wine cellar!'

There was a short pause while Ed wondered how to begin. There had been an inexplicably disturbing awareness between them that night in his kitchen, and he was sure she must have felt it too. It made things a bit awkward now, though. He didn't want to refer to it, but neither could he pretend that she had never come round.

It was the reason he had put off seeing Perdita until now, although it was also true that she ran an efficient and effective department. Ed had been hoping that either the memory of that awareness would fade—no luck there—or that seeing her at work would change things once more.

Looking at her now, he was only partly reassured. The quiet empathy he had felt sitting at the kitchen table had vanished, and Perdita was back to her peppy, punchy form. On the other hand, now that he had seen her in his home and knew that beneath the pizzazz she could be warm and sympathetic and honest, and had cares and concerns and stresses of her own, it was much harder to think of her as just another business colleague.

Although it was clear that was all she wanted to be. The more vulnerable side of Perdita was tucked firmly away behind a brisk façade of professionalism that Ed was fairly sure was designed to keep him at a distance and demonstrate that if she had been conscious of that unlikely awareness last week, she most certainly didn't want to be reminded of it.

Which was fair enough, Ed had to admit to himself. It wasn't likely that Perdita herself would ever be interested in a dull, middle-aged widower with three teenagers in tow.

Was it?

CHAPTER FOUR

ED CLEARED his throat. Well, no point going there. He'd better begin.

'So, did it take you long to recover from the leadership development course?' he asked. It felt pretty lame, but he had to start somewhere. This was the kind of meeting he could do in his sleep normally, but somehow everything felt different with Perdita.

'It wasn't too bad,' she said. 'It took me some time to catch up with things afterwards, and I got very sick of my colleagues screeching and pretending to be peacocks whenever I appeared,' she added tartly, 'but, apart from that, it was OK.'

He was leaning forward, resting his forearms on his knees and letting his loosely clasped hands fall easily between them as the penetrating grey eyes rested on her face. 'What did you think of the course?' he asked.

Realising that she was fiddling with the file on her lap, Perdita made herself stop and rest her hands on top of it.

'Honestly? I thought all the animal stuff was a bit silly, but it's been quite useful in trying to recognise that different members of my team have different strengths. And I learnt how to build a pontoon bridge, so it wasn't all bad!'

He smiled in a way that did horrible things to her heart-beat. 'You never know when that will come in handy! You weren't that impressed by the course when you were there, as I remember, but I'm glad you got something out of it.'

He paused and his expression became more serious. 'I do have some feedback from the facilitators for you but, before we discuss that, I'd like to know how you envisage your role at Bell Browning developing.'

'In what respect?' asked Perdita cautiously. She didn't like the sound of feedback.

'Are you happy as Operations Manager?'

'Yes,' she said, suspicious about where all this was going. 'Is there a problem with my performance?'

'On the contrary,' said Ed, picking up a file from the seat next to him and scanning it. 'Operations have an excellent reputation for delivering on time and under cost. Congratulations. The Board are very pleased with what you've done since you took over.'

'It's not just me,' said Perdita quickly. 'Everyone on the team has worked really hard—and that's in spite of me being a peacock,' she couldn't resist adding.

The grey eyes glinted distractingly. 'Clearly your leadership style works. What was it again? "I tell my staff what to do and they do it"?' Ed's voice was threaded with amusement.

Perdita had the grace to blush. 'I do try and be a little more tactful than that most of the time.'

'And your staff speak very highly of you too.' Ed closed the file and dropped it on to the table between them. 'The question is whether you want to stay as Operations Manager or if you'd like to develop your role further.'

'In what way?' Perdita's gaze sharpened with interest and she sat up straighter.

'I've been in discussion with the Board and we see the potential to expand internationally,' he said. 'We'd need someone with a specific responsibility for liaising with prospective clients overseas, and your languages and experience of working overseas make you the ideal candidate. This is still at the discussion stage, of course, but it would be useful to know if you would be interested in principle.'

Ed was somewhat taken aback to see Perdita light up like a candle with excitement. For a moment she seemed to shimmer with such energy that he actually blinked, but the next moment the expressive eyes were clouding over. 'In principle, yes, of course I would be interested,' she said slowly, 'but it depends how much travelling would be involved.'

'I imagine you would need to make some visits overseas,' Ed said carefully, and saw her face fall. 'Why, would that be a problem?'

'It probably would be.' Perdita struggled to swallow her disappointment. It wasn't fair! Her dream job, dangled in front of her and then whisked away before she even had a chance to fantasise about it! But there was no point in not being realistic. 'I may not be a parent,' she said, 'but that doesn't mean I don't have other responsibilities. I have to consider my mother. I don't think I could go away and leave her on her own now.'

'Even if you had care arrangements in place?'

Perdita shook her head despondently. 'She won't accept anything like that, certainly not at the moment.' From somewhere she mustered a smile—cool, professional, not at all the smile of someone who felt like bursting into tears and wailing, It's not *fair!* At least she hoped it wasn't, but she had never been renowned for hiding her feelings.

'Thank you for thinking of me,' she said, just like a real

grown-up, 'but I have to be honest with you. Obviously, I would love the challenge of a job like that, but I don't think I would be able to take it on right now.'

'That's a pity,' said Ed, meaning it. 'Still, we're only at the planning stage and it may be that things will change. We don't need to make any immediate decisions in any case.'

There was a tiny pause. Perdita was having a job to keep the smile on her face. Disappointment gnawed at her. She had been feeling restless recently, and the prospect of a new and interesting job would have been just what she needed to banish the increasingly suffocating feeling of being trapped in Ellsborough. It wouldn't be fair to blame her mother. *She* was the one who had chosen to come back home and she had tried to make the best of it, making a place for herself at Bell Browning. Without Nick, her career was really all she had, Perdita realised, and now it looked as if even that would have to take second place to her other responsibilities.

Suppressing a sigh, she began to get to her feet. 'Well, if that's everything…?' she said, smoothing down her skirt, but Ed held up a hand.

'Not quite,' he said, and Perdita subsided back into her seat at the note in his voice. 'We still need to discuss the feedback from the leadership development course.'

'Oh, that.' She had a feeling she wasn't going to enjoy this.

'Yes, *that*,' Ed agreed, a suspicious glint in his eyes. He pulled a sheet of paper from the file on the table and skimmed through it. 'It makes for interesting reading! There's no doubt about your abilities, Perdita, but your approach to both clients and colleagues can be—how shall I put it?—let's say a little *forthright*. Not to put too fine a point on it,' he said, 'the feeling is that some of your sharp edges need to be knocked off.'

'What sharp edges?' demanded Perdita. Sharply, in fact.

'Perhaps you need to be a little bit more aware of how other people are reacting in certain situations,' he said carefully. 'You've got a great ability to enthuse people and sweep them along with you, but sometimes—especially when you're communicating with senior executives—situations require a certain sensitivity. Those are the times when telling people what to do and then expecting them to do it just won't work!'

Perdita opened her mouth to snap at him, and then closed it again just in time. 'What exactly are you proposing?' she asked coldly instead.

Ed leaned back in his chair and scrutinised her indignant face. 'Bell Browning is an important employer in Ellsborough,' he said, 'but as far as I'm aware the firm hasn't shown much awareness of corporate social responsibility. I want to get everyone more involved in the community, and there are a number of projects that I think we can be usefully associated with.'

'Right,' said Perdita, who was beginning to get impatient. She hated long discussions and liked to get immediately to the point, but Ed clearly wasn't going to be hurried.

'One of those is an urban regeneration scheme that's just starting on wasteland in Booker Street, just down the road from here.'

Perdita only just forbore from glancing at her watch. What did all this have to do with feedback? 'Is that building affordable housing?' she asked, belatedly realising that Ed was waiting for her to pretend an interest.

'Partly, yes, but an important part of the project is creating an environment that is part park, part community garden, where people can grow vegetables and fruit, or just enjoy their own green space with trees and flowers. The idea is that it will be a place where the whole community can come together eventually, and it's hoped that as many as possible will be involved in transforming the wasteland into something beautiful. In particular, it will be an opportunity for teenagers who have been in trouble with the police for one reason or another—petty crimes or antisocial behaviour—to put something back into the community.'

'You mean it's a kind of community service?'

'In some ways. Most of them will probably be sentenced to work a certain number of hours in the garden, but by doing that they'll have the opportunity to learn about teamwork and the satisfaction of creating something out of nothing.'

Perdita couldn't imagine any of the teenagers she knew finding much satisfaction in gardening, but she wisely kept her thoughts to herself. She had been rather too free with her opinions with Ed in the past, and look where it had got her—a reputation for 'sharp edges'!

'I haven't heard of this project,' she said to show that she was still listening.

'You will,' said Ed. 'It's the brainchild of an Ellsborough garden designer. I met her a couple of days ago. Grace is an inspiring woman,' he told Perdita thoughtfully. 'She can't be much more than thirty, but her husband died tragically last year and she's decided to set up a trust in his memory to develop the garden project. She's passionate about plants and what working on the land can teach all of us, and about the need to give some of these troubled kids a sense of being rooted in the community.'

Poor Grace, being a widow so young, Perdita thought, although she wasn't convinced about her gardening obsession. Surely there were easier ways to remember her husband? Perdita herself had never had any interest in gardening and didn't propose to start now. Plus, she couldn't help feeling a bit miffed that Ed had taken the time to meet 'passionate' Grace rather than his sharp-edged Operations Manager. He certainly seemed very taken with her.

Perdita's lips tightened. What or who was Ed passionate about? Nothing, probably, she thought huffily, still sulking about being passed over in favour of the oh-so-inspiring Grace.

Then her eyes dropped to his mouth and she changed her mind. She didn't know what would stir him to passion, but there was something about that cool, quiet mouth that made her wish that she did. Just looking at it set a dangerous warmth spilling through her, and she wrenched her eyes away with an effort.

Enough. Whatever made Ed passionate, it certainly wasn't *her*.

'What's all this got to do with me?' she asked, more brusquely than she had intended.

'I want you to spend a couple of hours every week working with these kids on the garden project.'

Perdita stared at him, aghast. 'Me? But I don't know anything about gardening! Or teenagers, come to that!'

'You won't be there to teach them. It'll be a learning experience for you too.'

'But—'

'I know it'll be a challenge, but you're someone who responds to challenges. I saw the way you pulled everyone together on those team tasks in the rain that day. This will be harder, but I think you'll get a lot out of it.'

'Oh, *do* you?' Perdita's eyes narrowed dangerously. 'And if I tell you that I haven't got time to mess around in a garden with a lot of antisocial kids?'

Ed's cool grey gaze met her angry brown one quite steadily. 'I need you to make time,' he said quite quietly, but there was a note of finality in his voice and an uncompromising set to his mouth that gave her pause.

She scowled, sensing that she was beaten but unwilling to admit it. 'I hate getting my hands dirty,' she grumbled. 'And I just don't see that this project of yours will make any difference at all to how I work. Either you think I can do the job or you don't! Ken Fowler would never have bullied staff into doing something that they didn't want to do,' she added unwisely.

'Ken isn't Chief Executive any more,' Ed pointed out, an edge of steel in his voice. 'I am. And I want a team that is open to new challenges and new experiences, and who won't whine when they're asked to do something new!'

'Will all the dolphins and owls in the company be sent to work in the garden as well?' Perdita asked tightly.

'No, that wouldn't be a challenge for them. But they'll be asked to contribute to the community in some other way. The point of that course was that we learnt something about ourselves and how we can develop as individuals, and we can only do that by stretching ourselves, and challenging ourselves to deal with situations that are naturally uncomfortable for us.'

'Do panthers have to stretch themselves too, or are they above that kind of thing?'

For a moment Perdita wondered if she might have gone too far. Ed was her boss, after all, and he was unlikely to take kindly to sarcasm, but then he smiled.

'No, I get to be challenged too. I have to learn to be more intuitive and more open emotionally, apparently. Believe me,' he said as he got to his feet, signalling that the meeting was at an end, 'that will be as hard for me as working with teenagers will be for you!'

'I can't *believe* I'm going to have to go and work in some grotty garden,' Perdita grumbled to her friend that night. Millie's teenagers were both out and she had seized on the chance to meet Perdita for a drink.

'It might not be that bad,' said Millie, who had an infuriating tendency to look on the bright side of everything. 'Some people find gardening very therapeutic.'

'This gardening won't be! Ed wouldn't be sending me if there was any chance I would have a good time.' Perdita took a defiant gulp of her wine. 'No, he wants it to be as tough as possible for me. He wants to crush my spirit, in fact,' she finished dramatically.

Millie remained annoyingly unmoved at the dreadful prospect of seeing her friend crushed and beaten. 'I doubt that,' she said placidly. 'It sounded to me as if he wanted you to get a bit more experience of dealing with people who aren't used to doing what you tell them, and I've got to say that putting you in with a bunch of teenagers with antisocial behaviour orders is the best experience you could have! If you can deal with them, you can deal with anyone!'

'Well, I think it's a waste of time, just like that stupid course,' said Perdita crossly. 'Who does Edward Merrick think he is?'

'He thinks he's your chief executive,' Millie said. 'Oh, and actually, he *is*! That makes him your boss.' She pointed a warning finger at her friend. 'If you had any sense, you'd be sucking up to him, not telling him he's stupid and refusing to do things his way.'

'I've got no intention of sucking up to Edward Merrick,'

said Perdita, outraged at the very idea. 'I've already given him a bottle of Dad's best wine, and what does he do? Send me to wallow around in mud once a week!'

Millie eyed her friend thoughtfully. 'He sounded nice from what you told me about him turning out to be your mother's neighbour. I got the feeling you were quite taken with him, in fact.'

'Well, I'm not!' snapped Perdita, pushing those odd tingles of attraction and her stupid nervousness earlier that day firmly out of her mind.

How could she be taken with a man who'd dangled her perfect job in front of her nose and had then proceeded to send her out to grub around some wasteland and no doubt get absolutely filthy just so he could salve his social conscience? If Ed was so keen to save the world, let him go and dig.

She drained her glass with an air of defiance. 'He's my boss, that's all,' she said. 'I don't even like him.'

Perdita turned up her collar and regarded the wasteland with a mixture of disbelief and distaste. A garden? Here? Surely there must be some mistake, she decided. Or was it possible that the whole thing was an elaborate hoax contrived by Ed and Grace Dunn just to get her out the office on a cold, damp Thursday afternoon and fill her with dismay at the thought of working in this horrible pile of rubbish, mud and old bricks?

Grace had emailed her earlier in the week to suggest that she came along today at half past three for an introductory session, and to wear her oldest clothes as she was likely to get very dirty. Having already sacrificed her favourite boots to Ed Merrick's notion of leadership training, Perdita had no intention of ruining anything else. Grudgingly, she had invested in a fleece and a pair of rubber boots, and she had changed into her oldest pair of jeans at the office, stalking out to the car park with her fiercest glare in place in case anyone had the nerve to mock her for her change of style. She had managed to get through forty years perfectly well without owning a fleece, and would happily have managed another forty if it hadn't been for Edward Merrick!

She was *so* over her attraction for him! He and Grace were probably lurking in that hut right now, sniggering behind their hands at her expression, Perdita thought vengefully as she picked her way towards it through the mud.

She didn't know whether she would rather it was a big joke or for real. Either way, she was far too busy to be wasting time out in this dump. She liked projects with achievable goals, but the idea of creating a garden here was clearly unfeasible. She couldn't imagine what Grace Dunn was thinking about. She must be a fool or a fantasist, Perdita decided roundly.

But Grace didn't look like a fool when she welcomed Perdita into the hut, which was larger and brighter and a lot cleaner inside than it had looked from outside. She was a slight, very pretty woman with luminous grey eyes and a cloud of dishevelled hair, but her handshake was firm and it soon became clear that she had both intelligence and authority in spite of her youth. Eyeing her critically, Perdita thought that Ed had been right. She could only be in her early thirties—very young to be a widow, certainly.

There was no sign of Ed in the hut, which was partly a relief, although that was swiftly replaced by panic as Perdita found herself being introduced to a group of morose youths. What on earth was she doing here? She knew nothing about teenagers, other than what she had learnt from friends like Millie, and that was enough to convince her that the chances of her having anything in common with them were close to nil.

More intimidated than she wanted to admit, Perdita sat on the edge of the semicircle of chairs. She didn't feel much of a peacock in this company, she thought, eyeing the others from under her lashes. They looked uniformly sullen and truculent, and about as pleased to be there as she felt.

Grace took charge. 'You're probably all wondering what you're doing here,' she said, 'so I'm going to show you.' She unveiled an artist's impression of a cross between a park and a garden, with separate areas for growing fruit and vegetables, and for adventure playgrounds. 'You're here to make this,' she said.

Perdita could only gape at the picture. 'No way!' said a boy next to her, surprised out of his sulky silence, and she couldn't help nodding in agreement. Maybe she had more in common with teenagers than she thought. At least this boy could see that what Grace proposed was impossible.

But Grace was having none of it. 'You'll see,' she said. 'Our first job is to clear the ground and prepare it in time for planting. It may not seem very exciting, but this stage is one of the most important in the whole project.'

Perhaps realising that they remained deeply sceptical, Grace didn't waste much time trying to convince them all, and issued everyone instead with a gardening fork and a pair of work gloves. Perdita found herself allocated to clear a patch of ground with a monosyllabic boy called Tom who hid his face behind a fall of tousled hair and apparently communicated only in grunts.

Cleverly, Grace had also pointed out that they would always work on the same area at first so they would be able to measure their progress against the others. What effect this had on Tom was doubtful, but Perdita's competitive spirit was immediately roused and she immediately vowed that their ground would be cleared faster and better than anyone else's.

Since she was here, she reasoned, she might as well make a success of it.

The truth was that Perdita didn't know any other way to tackle a job other than to do it well, and preferably to beat everyone else while she was at it.

She glanced at the boy beside her. 'Well, we might as well start,' she said.

Morosely, he bent to pick up a rusty can, but the effort seemed to exhaust him and he stood holding it as if he couldn't work out how it had come to be in his hand.

'Look, it'll take ages if we try to pick up all this rubbish piece by piece,' said Perdita, exasperated. The ground was littered with broken concrete, rusty metal, tattered plastic, broken bottles and discarded fast food packaging, and she eyed it with distaste. 'Let's use the forks to pull it into piles and then try to get rid of it.'

She didn't care if that was her being bossy. It would be enough of a challenge for her just to get through the afternoon here, let alone try and remember to be inclusive and non-confrontational.

It was harder work than Perdita had imagined, and she thought vengefully about Ed as she struggled to make a dent in the mess. The more rubbish she scraped away, the more appeared in its place. Clearing this place was like one of those mythological labours the Greek gods were so good at thinking up, and maybe that made her a heroine—albeit one badly in need of a magic trick to help her out—but frankly she would rather be at the office, catching up on her paperwork.

How was this supposed to knock off her sharp edges? Perdita wondered bitterly. She could feel herself getting sharper by the minute. Ed Merrick was no doubt comfortably ensconced in his warm office thinking up other forms of torture for his staff. She should start a rebellion, she thought, forking darkly through the rubbish. Let him see what he thought about staff development *then*!

She had hardly seen Ed since their meeting, which was probably just as well as there was no way she was going to take Millie's advice and start sucking up to him. There were already more than enough people doing that, judging by the gossip she heard in the office. They had all dreaded his arrival in case it would mean swingeing cuts and changes but so far Ed had proved remarkably popular.

Perdita's secretary, Valerie, source of most information, raved about him until Perdita was sick of hearing about Ed this, Ed that. She wished he would stop being so inclusive and insisted that they all call him Mr Merrick instead. It would be a lot easier to dislike him if he turned out to be arrogant and ruthless or even pompous, but no! Ed appeared unable to put a foot wrong…except when dealing with his Operations Manager, clearly. As far as she could tell, Perdita herself was the only person with any reservations about him at all, and she couldn't help feeling a little aggrieved. Why wasn't he trying to win *her* over like everyone else?

They rarely coincided at work. Ed seemed happy to let her get on with her job, which she was pleased about—*obviously*—but he might have the decency to show a little interest in they were what doing in Operations, Perdita couldn't help thinking. The previous Chief Executive had always been summoning her to pointless meetings, but Ed seemed to have taken things to the other extreme.

Perdita sniffed disapprovingly as she forked up a motley collection of rusty cans. Ed might like to consider a slightly more hands-on approach some time. He was supposed to be running the company after all.

She had, in fact, been asked to attend a meeting in the Board Room on Tuesday, and the expectation of seeing Ed there had produced a nauseating combination of squirming and fluttering in her stomach as she'd made her way upstairs, only to find that he had asked his deputy to chair the meeting and wasn't even there. At which point an absurd sense of disappointment had sent her poor stomach into a nosedive, as if it didn't have enough to contend with.

Of course, when Perdita had visited her mother she had seen the lights on next door, but she could hardly go and knock again without a very good excuse. Ed would start to think she was some kind of stalker.

And anyway she didn't *want* to see him, Perdita reminded herself as she disentangled a torn and rancid carrier bag from her fork with a grimace of distaste, very glad that she was wearing gloves. Hadn't she told Millie that she didn't even like him?

All right, that probably wasn't *strictly* true, she acknowledged, dragging her fork furiously over the ground once more. She might as well be honest with herself. The truth was that she didn't want to like Ed because she didn't want to find him attractive, and she didn't want to find him attractive because she was afraid of getting involved with a father again.

Loving Nick, being hurt by him, had taught her a hard lesson. Sometimes the pain of his rejection still crept up and grabbed her by the throat, shaking her until she could hardly breathe because it hurt so much, even after all this time. Then she would feel again the cruel twist of her heart, the dull ache that had been part of her for so many months. She had spent two years trying to fit in with Nick's priorities as a father, and in the end it had almost destroyed her. She wouldn't—couldn't—go through that again.

Ed was a father, so she wasn't interested.

And he wasn't interested in her, it seemed.

Right. Funny how that didn't make her feel better.

When they had gathered two large piles of rubbish, Perdita stopped and straightened, holding a hand to her back. She would be lucky if she could walk tomorrow.

'Right, time for a reward,' she said to Tom. Digging in her pocket, she found a Mars bar that she had grabbed from the vending machine on the way out in lieu of lunch.

It had been Perdita's idea to work in strips. When they had done one each and gathered all the mess into piles they could have a treat, she had suggested. Half a Mars bar wasn't much of a treat compared to, say, a hot bath with a glass of champagne, which was all she really wanted right then, but it was better than nothing.

And it was chocolate, after all.

'Here,' she said, breaking the bar in two and handing half to Tom. 'Your reward.'

'Thanks,' he said as he took it. 'I'm starving.'

'What are you doing here?' asked Perdita curiously. In spite of his hunched shoulders, messy hair and the ubiquitous drab teenage uniform, he was quite well-spoken when he forgot to grunt, and someone had obviously taught him some manners along the way. Nor did he seem a likely candidate for an antisocial behaviour order that had brought most of the others to the garden project.

'I was sent,' he said.

'Why?' OK, maybe she was nosy, but she was allowed to be interested in people, wasn't she?

Tom shrugged. 'Bad attitude.' He glanced at Perdita from beneath his hair. 'What about you?'

'Same, I suppose,' said Perdita, chewing on her Mars bar, and he was betrayed into a laugh.

'*You?* Bad attitude?'

'Apparently I'm too sharp. They sent me from work.' She licked chocolate from her thumb. 'My boss is an arrogant, pretentious tyrant who thinks the experience will be good for me!'

'My dad thinks the same thing,' confessed Tom.

Perdita snorted. 'I notice that neither of them are actually here benefiting from the experience of clearing rubbish in the rain though, are they?'

'No,' he agreed, evidently warming to her. 'We should suggest they have a go next week.'

'I don't know about your dad, but I can't see me getting very far if I tried that on my boss.' She sighed as the faint drizzle grew heavier until it was unmistakably rain. 'When does this purgatory end?'

'Dad's picking me up at five o'clock.'

'That probably means that I have to stay here until then too. Oh, well.' She rubbed her aching back. 'We might as well start another strip…'

CHAPTER FIVE

BY THE time they got to the end of their third strip it was raining steadily and they were both sweaty with exertion, soaking wet and liberally splattered with mud. Perdita's hair was hanging in rats' tails and she paused to push her fringe back from her forehead with the back of her arm, pleased to notice that they had achieved far more than anyone else. Still, the challenge of being the best was beginning to wear thin.

'I wish your dad would turn up,' she told Tom. 'That would mean it's time to go.'

'There he is now,' said Tom, and Perdita wiped the drips from her eyes and peered in the direction of his pointing finger.

A man was heading towards them across the wasteland, hunched slightly against the rain. There was something familiar about his walk, Perdita thought. Something about the set of his shoulders and the way his presence drew the eye.

Something that set Perdita's heart bumping in a downward spiral.

'*That's* your father?' she asked in a hollow voice, and Tom looked at her in surprise. Her expression made him look towards his father and then back to Perdita with sudden understanding.

'That's your *boss*?' he said and, when he grinned, Perdita

could suddenly see his father in him. 'Don't worry,' he said, lowering his voice conspiratorially, 'I won't tell! Hi, Dad!' he called.

Ed squinted through the rain at his son, who seemed unnaturally cheery, and he lifted a hand in greeting. His keen gaze took in Tom and then moved to Perdita, standing next to him. In contrast to her usual immaculately groomed appearance, she was looking distinctly grubby and bedraggled but there was the same unmistakable sparkiness about her. Her eyes were bright, her skin glowing and she seemed to vibrate with energy in the middle of the dreary wasteland. Even Tom looked energised by her and was unconsciously mirroring the way Perdita stood with her fork planted firmly in front of her.

'You both look very wet!' he said, unable to prevent a smile as he looked from one to the other.

'Yes, and whose fault is that?' demanded Perdita snippily.

'Don't try and tell me that you haven't enjoyed yourself, Perdita,' said Ed. 'Grace says you and Tom have been working like dogs all afternoon. You've done twice as much as anyone else!'

Tom looked over to where the others were trailing back to hand in their forks, obviously realising for the first time that he had been working harder than anyone else. 'I didn't realise that it was a competition,' he said, and his father grinned.

'I'll bet it was for Perdita! Am I right?' he asked her.

Perdita put up her chin. She didn't like it when he laughed at her, but she was too honest to deny it.

'You probably would have had an easier time with another partner,' she admitted to Tom, but he just hunched a shoulder.

'You were cool,' he muttered.

Ed regarded him thoughtfully for a moment. 'Perdita works for Bell Browning as well,' he told Tom as they turned and headed for the exit. 'Her mother lives next door to us. She very kindly brought that bottle of wine I wouldn't waste on you the first night we moved in.'

'I remember,' Tom said with a shade of sulkiness. 'He wouldn't even let us taste it,' he told Perdita. 'He said it was too good for us.'

'Next time, I'll bring a cheap bottle of plonk,' she said with a laugh, and Tom brightened.

'You're coming again?'

'Oh, no...I only meant...' Perdita was deeply flustered by Tom's question. 'I was joking,' she tried to explain.

'I hope you will come again, though,' said Ed. 'In fact, why don't you come to supper? What do you think, Tom?'

'Cool,' said Tom.

That was just what Perdita had been afraid of. After her stupid comment and Tom's reaction, Ed obviously felt that he didn't have much choice but to invite her, but if he had wanted her to go to supper, he could have asked her before now.

'No, honestly,' she said, horribly embarrassed but doing her best to laugh it off . 'When I said next time, I really *didn't* mean to invite myself! It was just a figure of speech,' she finished lamely.

'I know, but come anyway,' said Ed, and smiled at her in a way that made the breath clog in her throat, and *that* made her heart batter in panic in case it was going to run out of oxygen. It wasn't fair that one smile could have such an alarming effect. 'The honest truth is that the kids are bored of being stuck with me—'

'We are!' Tom put in.

'—and I could do with some adult company, so we'd all

really appreciate it if you'd come,' finished Ed, pretending to cuff his son over the head.

He was being charming about it, given that he'd been placed in such an awkward position.

Perdita hesitated. What could she say? 'That would be lovely,' she decided in the end. No date had been suggested, so her answer was sufficiently vague for Ed to feel no obligation to follow the invitation up.

'What about tonight?'

'Tonight?' Having expected to be fobbed off with something equally vague, like a promise to be in touch or to arrange a date soon, Perdita was completely thrown by Ed's swift comeback.

'Isn't Thursday one of the nights you visit your mother?'

'Well, yes, it is…' How did he know that?

'You've been under observation,' Ed answered her unspoken question with a grin. 'Lauren spends a lot of time mooching in her room, which looks out over the drives, so she's our main source of information on your movements.'

'Dad,' said Tom, mortified by his father's revelation. 'You make us sound like a bunch of weirdos spying on her!'

'We're not weirdos,' Ed said. 'It's just that we haven't got enough distraction at the moment and Perdita's visits next door are the most exciting things that happen to us at the moment!'

His face was straight, but the grey eyes gleamed with amusement in a way that reminded Perdita vividly of the first time they had met.

She couldn't help laughing. 'Well, I'm glad to know that my life seems exciting to somebody!' she said.

'It does, so bring a bit of excitement into our lives and come for supper,' Ed urged. 'It won't be anything fancy.'

'You can say that again!' said Tom with a snort. 'Dad doesn't do fancy.'

No, Ed wouldn't do fancy, Perdita thought, studying him from under her lashes. He would cook the way he did everything else—capably, steadily, straightforwardly.

Would he make love that way, too?

The thought caught her unawares, grabbing her from behind and startling her so that she actually stumbled. She recovered almost immediately, but she was shaken, less by the unexpected question that had popped into her head than by her instant, instinctive conviction that no, Ed wouldn't make love like that. You only had to look at that mouth, and those hands, to know that he would be slow and sure and sensuous and—

And that was quite enough. Perdita was horrified at herself. What was she *thinking*?

Sending up a prayer of thanks that neither of them appeared to be mind-readers, she forced a smile.

'What *does* he do?' she asked Tom.

'Sausages and mash. Pasta bake. Roast chicken. Spaghetti bolognaise.'

'Hey, I can do more than that,' Ed objected mildly. 'I made a casserole the other day, remember?'

'It was gross. You're not making that again.'

Perdita suppressed a smile. She was feeling more under control now. 'I love spag bol.'

'You wouldn't if you had to eat it twice a week, every week,' muttered Tom, but Ed overrode him.

'Excellent, spaghetti bolognaise it is—and I'll try and provide a bottle of wine to rival the one you brought last time.'

'Well…' said Perdita, weakening. She was wet through and the thought of somebody else doing the cooking for once was very appealing. What was the harm, after all? There was no question of it being a date.

'In that case, I'd love to come,' she said. 'I'll have to give my mother something to eat first, but she should be settled by eight.'

'Great.' Ed smiled his unfair smile again as they reached the hut where Grace was collecting the gardening forks and gloves. 'We'll see you then.'

The first thing Perdita did when she got home was to run a deep, hot bath and she sighed with pleasure as she slid down beneath the bubbles. This was what she had been fantasising about as she'd scraped up all that disgusting rubbish, minus the glass of champagne, of course. She didn't want to have anything to drink before she drove.

And anyway, she didn't need champagne. She already felt as if a magnum of the stuff was fizzing along her veins and bubbling into her heart. The shameful truth was that she was ridiculously excited about the prospect of her simple supper.

Don't be so silly, Perdita told herself sternly. It was only a bowl of pasta, for heaven's sake! Hardly a heavy date with three teenagers in tow. But still she found herself throwing open the doors of her wardrobe and studying the contents with a frown. What *did* you wear when your boss invited you to eat spaghetti bolognaise with his kids? There ought to be some kind of protocol for these things, Perdita decided.

Normally she had a sure sense of her own style, but for some reason this occasion had her in a dither. It took her four attempts at getting dressed before she settled finally on a pair of loose trousers with a silk knit top, and she was thoroughly disgusted with herself for making such a fuss by then.

In spite of her determination to treat the whole thing in a casual spirit, her heart was pattering frantically against her ribs as she drove over to her mother's house.

The last time she had seen her mother, Helen James had been quite bright, but today her mood was querulous and snappy. She barely tasted the fish Perdita had bought to tempt her appetite before she pushed it away.

'I'll have it for lunch tomorrow.'

It would be ruined the next day, even supposing her mother remembered to heat it up correctly. Perdita looked at her mother worriedly as she picked up the plate. 'Aren't you feeling well?'

'I'm absolutely fine,' Helen snapped. 'For heaven's sake, stop *fussing*!'

'But you haven't had a good meal for ages.'

'I'm not hungry.'

Perdita drew a breath, then pulled out a chair and sat down opposite her mother. 'Mum, don't you think it's time you thought about getting someone in to help? It doesn't have to be a permanent arrangement, just someone to help with the cooking and cleaning until you feel better.'

'I *am* better, and I've already got a perfectly adequate cleaner. You know that Mrs Clements comes in twice a week.'

'I know you like Mrs Clements, Mum,' Perdita acknowledged with a sigh. Mrs Clements was the bane of her life at the moment. As far as Perdita could see, she did nothing but drink coffee and complain about not feeling very well whenever she came round, and it was the surest sign of her mother's decline that she wasn't prepared to brook any criticism of her cleaner, who never seemed to do any cleaning at all.

Perdita dug out a cloth and took out her feelings on the mess on top of the kitchen worktops. 'Wasn't she supposed to come today?' she asked, wrinkling her nose with distaste as she rinsed out the cloth.

'She did come.'

'Where did she clean?' It certainly hadn't been the kitchen!

'Where she usually does,' Helen said sharply. 'And you're not to say anything else to her, Perdita,' she warned in some agitation before her daughter could retort. 'She was very upset after last time.'

Perdita counted to ten, very slowly, before she could trust herself to reply. 'I'm not suggesting that Mrs Clements doesn't come any more, just that someone else could drop in about midday to make sure you have some lunch and—'

She stopped as she saw the old familiar stubborn look settle on her mother's face. 'I don't want strangers in the house, Perdita,' she said. 'I'm perfectly capable of looking after myself.'

Then why was *she* here, cooking and washing and cleaning? Perdita wanted to stand up and shout at her mother, but she wrung out the cloth and attacked the worktops once more instead. Her mood of excited anticipation had been steadily trickling away since she'd arrived, leaving her with the usual mixture of frustration and guilty resentment. That champagne feeling had definitely gone flat.

By the time Perdita had settled her mother in front of the television and finished clearing up, it was ten past eight and her mood had plummeted. She was tired after the unaccustomed physical activity this afternoon, and now she was tense and cross too. The last thing she wanted was an evening of small talk. She would knock on Ed's door and explain that she really needed to go straight home. She didn't suppose Ed would care particularly.

Ed answered the door, took one look at her face and, before Perdita had a chance to make her apologies, he had stepped back to usher her inside. 'You need a glass of wine,' he said. 'Come into the kitchen.'

Perdita was suddenly too tired to argue. It had been a long day, with one thing and another, and in the face of Ed's calm acceptance she knew with appalled certainty that if she started to explain her frustration and guilt she would start to cry, and she couldn't let herself do that.

He didn't seem to expect her to say anything, so she followed him into the kitchen and sat down at the table while he poured her a glass of wine.

'I'll just get on with supper,' he said, pushing the glass towards her. 'You drink that.'

Obediently, Perdita picked up the glass. A CD player had been set up since she had last been there, and there was restful classical music playing in the background. She sipped her wine and watched Ed move around the kitchen, intensely grateful that he wasn't asking her to talk. A tea towel was flung over his shoulder and his movements were unhurried and competent and insensibly calming: washing lettuce, opening the fridge in search of Parmesan, chopping tomatoes, stirring his simmering sauce, setting a big pan of water to boil...

The kitchen was warm and the sauce smelt wonderful, the music was soothing and the wine cool and crisp, just the way she liked it, but it was Ed's quiet, steadying presence that made Perdita's knotted muscles in her shoulders gradually relax as her tension dissipated.

'Thank you—' she broke the silence at last with a sigh '—I needed that.'

'I know.' Ed gave the bolognaise sauce a final stir, tapped the wooden spoon on the side of the pan and balanced it on the edge before turning to her with a smile. 'Have some more wine.'

Perdita let him top up her glass and then his own. 'I'm

afraid I'm not being a very good guest,' she told him as he pulled out a chair and sat down opposite her.

'You don't need to be,' said Ed. 'You just need to be here.'

In truth, he had been feeling a little guilty about the way he and Tom had made it impossible for her to refuse coming tonight. She hadn't seemed that keen, but he had suddenly really wanted to see her at his kitchen table again. Ed couldn't even explain why to himself, but he knew that he didn't want to wait and make some formal arrangement for the future. He would just be nervous then, and it would have seemed more like a date, and obviously neither of them wanted *that*.

No, it was just that the thought of sitting quietly with her, of talking and sharing a meal, had seemed inexplicably appealing all at once and, since Tom had provided the opening, Ed had taken his chance. He hadn't been lying when he'd said that he looked forward to some adult company. There were times when he could feel very alone, even with three children in the house. Perdita's presence the other evening had been somehow warming, revitalising, and he had wanted that again.

But the moment he'd opened the door, he had seen the strain on her face and had guessed that Perdita had given enough of herself for one evening. Perhaps, though, he could do something for her, even if it were just to let her sit without talking for a while.

'You're very understanding,' she said now, and Ed looked across the table at her. She was less glossy than usual. Her hair was tucked tiredly behind her ears and the chocolate-brown eyes were huge and dark, but, even weary and stressed, there was a vividness about her that illuminated the whole room.

'I know what it's like,' he told her. 'After Sue died, people were very kind, but sometimes what I really needed was just to sit quietly and not have to make an effort. The good friends were the ones who gave me a bit of time until I came round.

'Those first few months were mad. It felt like I was running desperately on one spot, just trying to keep on top of work, making sure that I was Jessica for the kids, trying to help them bear it and knowing that I couldn't make it better… Everyone kept advising me to stop and think about myself, but I couldn't just switch off like that. I'd just end up worrying about the girls and what was going to happen to them without a mother, how Tom would cope…I was the least of my worries.'

'It doesn't sound as if you had a chance to grieve yourself,' Perdita said, suspecting that he was talking so that she didn't have to. Ed was a kind man, she realised uneasily. After Nick, kindness was dangerously seductive, far harder to resist for a woman her age than any amount of bulging muscles.

'I didn't properly until nearly a year later,' he was saying. 'The kids and I had settled into a kind of routine, and I'd got very good at keeping everything bottled up. Looking back, I can see that I was completely rigid with tension and probably very difficult to live with, but I didn't realise until one of my oldest friends turned up with his wife one Friday. They just announced that Katie would stay with the kids and Mike was taking me walking in the Dales.'

Ed's mouth twisted in a wry smile at the memory. 'I didn't want to go, but Mike wouldn't take no for an answer and, as it turned out, it was exactly what I needed. We walked for miles, not really talking at all. It was the first chance I'd had to think about Sue and how much I missed her…'

He stopped, remembering how the grief he had kept tightly screwed down for so long had erupted without warning. 'We stopped for a rest on a limestone pavement up there at one point. It was a beautiful day and the view was fantastic…and I suddenly started to cry.'

Perdita's throat was tight. It was hard for men like Ed to admit that they cried, but she respected him the more for it. Sometimes it took a lot more strength to acknowledge pain or weakness than it did to bluff and bluster and pretend that feelings weren't important.

'Mike didn't tell me to pull myself together or pat my shoulder and say that it would be all right. He just sat there and wasn't embarrassed and, when I'd finished, he handed me a cup of coffee and apologised he didn't have anything stronger.'

'He sounds like a good friend.'

'The best,' said Ed. 'I was better after that.'

'I'm sorry,' she said inadequately. 'Does it still hurt as much?'

He shook his head. 'No, you get used to it, of course. Some times are worse than others.'

Perdita nodded. She knew what that was like. It had taken her a very long time to get over Nick. She would think that she was doing OK. At first a few days would go by, then weeks and latterly a whole month or so, when she hardly thought about him, but then the old misery would swamp her without warning and for no obvious reason, plunging her back into wretchedness of long hours spent fighting tears, of nights when she would wake in the early hours and lie alone in the darkness, churning with loss. That was when she would miss Nick so much she felt as if she were drowning in it, until she managed to drag herself out of it once more. Even now, two years later, the memory of how he had let her down when she'd most needed him still had the power to make her wince at odd moments.

'I miss Sue most when something's happened with the kids,' Ed said. 'If I'm worried about one of them, or if there's something to celebrate, it seems all wrong that she isn't there. I miss just being married too,' he went on slowly. 'I miss having someone to make plans with, someone to talk to at the end of the day, someone to hold…God, listen to me!' He broke off with a humorous roll of his eyes. 'I'm not usually this maudlin.'

'It must be lonely,' Perdita said, conscious of a strange pang of envy, mixed with guilt and disgust at herself. How could you envy a woman who was dead?

'Yes, it is sometimes,' said Ed, but not in a self-pitying way. Reaching across the table, he topped up Perdita's glass. 'What about you? Have you never wanted to be married?'

Perdita swirled the wine in her glass, studying it intently as if it held the answer. 'Once,' she admitted after a long pause. If Nick had ever asked her to marry him, of course she would have said yes. 'It didn't work out.' She shrugged, managed a smile as she lifted her eyes to Ed. 'It was probably for the best.'

'In what way?' he asked quietly, watching her face.

'Maybe if I'd met the right guy in my twenties…' Perdita was very conscious of his eyes on her, and she bent her eyes to her wine once more, swirling it mindlessly round and round. 'Maybe then I would have settled down, done the whole marriage-and-kids thing…but I didn't. I've had my share of relationships, and some of them were more fun than others, but there wasn't anyone I could really imagine wanting to wake up with every single morning.'

Except Nick, of course.

'And now I've been on my own too long,' she went on. 'I'm used to having my own space. I like being able to go home and close the door and do whatever I want, whenever I want, without consulting anyone else. I don't get lonely. I earn a good salary. I've got good friends, a nice flat, I can afford to travel… Why would I want to give up all that to get married?'

'No reason, unless you think of marriage as sharing rather than giving up your freedom.' Ed's voice was carefully neutral.

'Sharing means compromising,' said Perdita. 'I'm forty now. I'm set in my ways, and the chances are that anyone I meet is going to be too. Relationships are more complicated now. We've all got baggage—failed relationships, grief, disappointment, responsibilities—and that all has to be part of the compromise too. You have to really want someone to be prepared to compromise your whole life.'

'And you never have?'

Irritated by her own endless swirling, Perdita put her glass down with a click. 'Yes,' she said, her eyes sliding away from his. 'But he didn't want me enough to compromise, and a relationship takes two. You can't do it all on your own.'

'No,' said Ed, wondering what sort of man a woman like Perdita would love. What sort of man wouldn't love her enough to compromise even a little.

'So I've given up on compromise,' said Perdita, and she snapped on a bright smile. 'When I meet a man, I don't think about anything except having a good time, and when it's not fun any more, it's over.'

Well, that told him, Ed thought wryly. 'If you're happy to be on your own, I suppose that's the best attitude,' he said after a tiny pause.

'You obviously *don't* like being on your own.' For some reason, Perdita found herself wishing that she hadn't been quite so adamant about the joys of single life. 'Have you thought about getting married again?'

It was Ed's turn to play with his glass. 'When Sue knew that she was dying, she made me promise that I would move on and make a new life, try to find someone else, but it's easier said than done. For a long while I couldn't imagine being with anyone but her, and then, as time went on, I did think about what it might be like to find someone else but, between the kids and work, there hasn't been that much time to think about meeting the right woman,' he said dryly. 'Even supposing I knew who or what the right woman was! But Lauren is fourteen now, so she's getting more independent, and it means that I don't need to struggle to find an acceptable babysitter if I do want to go out in the evening. I'm hoping that moving here will make a difference to all of us.'

'Has it yet?'

'It's a bit soon to tell. In spite of moaning constantly about missing their friends, Cassie and Lauren already seem to have made new ones. Tom's finding it harder. He doesn't have their social skills.'

And you? Perdita wanted to ask. *What kind of woman would be the right one for you?*

'Tom was fine with me this afternoon,' she said instead, feeling that she was straying into very intimate territory. Perhaps it would be better to get back to more impersonal topics. 'I felt sorry for him being landed with an old bag like me instead of having one of the other kids as a partner, but he certainly didn't make it obvious.'

'I should hope not,' said Ed, evidently happy to follow her lead and steer the conversation back on to safer ground. 'I don't know what he thought at first—Tom's not exactly chatty, as you've probably gathered—but I doubt very much that he considered you an "old bag"! He liked you.'

'You didn't ask Grace to put us together, then?'

'Of course not. In spite of what my children think, I'm not that much of a control freak! I have to say that I was glad to see that he had been paired up with you, though. It meant he worked a lot harder than he would have done otherwise—swept along in your wake! I think he enjoyed it a lot more than he expected to, thanks to you.'

Perdita made a face. 'I don't know that "enjoy" was the operative word!'

'Oh, come on, Perdita, it wasn't *that* bad, was it?'

'It wasn't *quite* as bad as I was expecting,' was all she would acknowledge. 'I just can't see how the project is going to work, though.'

'Didn't Grace show you the plans?'

'Yes, but the project needs investment as well as a few people with forks,' she pointed out. 'It's a huge area—the hard landscaping alone will cost a fortune.'

Ed's mouth quirked in amusement. 'There speaks a practical businesswoman! But I agree. Substantial investment is going to be needed. Grace tells me that she's hoping to get sponsorship for all the materials and wants to persuade skilled craftsmen to volunteer to teach the kids how to lay bricks, make hedges and fences and that kind of thing.'

'It all sounds a bit vague to me,' said Perdita crisply, wondering when Ed had had all these cosy little chats with Grace and what else they had been talking about. 'Fund-raising takes a lot of time. Grace told *me* that she's organising all this from her front room at the moment and trying to run her own consultancy. She won't be able to keep that going indefinitely.'

'No,' Ed agreed, getting up to stir his sauce. 'Which is

why I've offered to sponsor the cost of getting someone to work part-time on the project, doing all the administration and chasing up potential sponsors. Grace thought that was a brilliant idea.'

He lifted the lid of the big saucepan to check whether the water had come up to the boil, while Perdita turned her glass crossly between her fingers. Ed and Grace seemed to have a mutual admiration society going. Good for them.

She scowled down into her wine, aware that she might not mind if Ed hadn't more or less admitted that he was looking for a new wife—or if she hadn't liked Grace so much. She was quite a bit younger than Ed, of course, but she was lovely and, as a widow, she would presumably have a lot in common with him. They were perfect for each other, in fact.

And why was *that* thought so depressing?

CHAPTER SIX

SOMETHING in the silence suddenly made Perdita lift her head to see that Ed had turned from the cooker and was patently waiting for her to answer a question that she had been too wrapped up in her thoughts to hear.

'Sorry?' she said awkwardly, a slight flush staining her cheeks.

'I was just wondering if you knew of anyone who might like a part-time job.'

'I might,' said Perdita, thinking of Millie, who had been struggling to make ends meet since her divorce. 'Would the hours be flexible?'

'I don't see why not, but it would be up to Grace. Get them to contact her if they're interested.'

Ed wiped his hands on the tea towel still draped over his shoulder and pulled open a drawer in search of cutlery. 'Supper's nearly ready. I'll just lay the table.'

'Let me do that.' Perdita pushed back her chair and stood up. 'I've just been sitting here doing nothing,' she said guiltily.

'You're a guest. That's your job,' said Ed, but he let her come round to take the spoons and forks from him.

Perdita's hands brushed his as she reached for the cutlery and a small, sharp thrill jolted through her at the touch so that she drew a breath that was dangerously close to a gasp. His skin was warm and she was acutely aware of how close he was. Afraid that he would read her response in her eyes, she didn't look at his face but found herself fixing on the rough cotton weave of his shirt, the way one of his buttons was chipped and how his neck rose in a strong column from his casual open collar. She could see the pulse beating in his throat and had a sudden, shocking impulse to press her lips to it.

Aghast at herself, Perdita turned sharply away, fumbling with the cutlery in her hands. Her heart was thumping so hard that she was finding it hard to breathe.

Ed evidently hadn't even registered that brief graze of their hands, or if he had it certainly hadn't bothered him. He had found some mats and was slinging them carelessly around the table.

'I usually insist that one of the kids lays the table,' he said as Perdita concentrated fiercely on setting a spoon and fork on either side of each mat, 'but as it tends to lead to a fight about whose turn it is and why I treat them as slaves I thought I'd spare you the aggro tonight. Sometimes it's easier just to do it yourself.'

Although her head was bent, Perdita could see his hands as he set everything else on the table. They were strong and square and capable, and every time they caught at the corner of her vision she felt hollow. God, she must pull herself together!

'This music is lovely,' she croaked, hating the breathless crack in her voice. 'What is it? Bach?'

'That's right.' She felt him glance at her. 'Do you like classical music?'

'I like it when I hear it, but I don't know anything about it at all. My father used to say I was a complete philistine.'

'That's what I say about Cassie, so perhaps there's hope for her yet.'

'There are masses of classical concerts in Ellsborough and I always say I'll go, but of course I never get round to it.'

Perdita could feel herself babbling and wished she had something else to do with her hands. There were only so many times one could straighten a fork. She sat back down instead and picked up her wine. 'I do enjoy it when I listen to it like now, though.'

'Well, make the most of it as it will probably end up being turned off when the kids come down,' said Ed wryly. He went to the door and bellowed, 'Supper's ready!' up the stairs.

'I'm surprised,' said Perdita, who had recovered a little. 'I'd have had you down as a man who listened to what he wanted in his own house.'

'I was before I came up against the immovable will of a teenager,' Ed said with grim humour. 'I could insist, I suppose, but there are so many fights with adolescents in the house that you end up choosing the ones you think are really important and letting all the others go.'

Sure enough, when Cassie clattered down the stairs the first thing she did as she swirled into the kitchen was to head for the CD player. 'Oh, Dad, not this boring old stuff again,' she said, ejecting the CD. 'You are so *sad*!'

'Perdita was enjoying that,' Ed pointed out mildly, but Cassie only tossed her head.

'She was probably just saying that to be polite. Can I put on some real music?'

'No,' said Ed as he drained the spaghetti. 'It's Bach or nothing.'

Rolling her eyes, Cassie plonked herself down next to

Perdita as Tom drifted into the room, followed by Lauren, who was a slighter, quieter version of her big sister.

'I can't do my stupid French homework,' she complained, slumping into a chair when she had been introduced to Perdita. 'I *hate* my teacher here. Everybody does.'

'Be nice to Perdita and maybe she'll help you afterwards,' said Ed. 'She speaks French.'

The three of them turned to look at her as if she had sprouted three heads. 'I spent a year working in Paris,' Perdita excused herself.

She expected Cassie to sneer at this but instead she seemed to be impressed and talked animatedly about a school trip to Paris the previous year. 'I wanted Dad to take us to France this summer but he wouldn't,' she told Perdita.

'I took you to France a couple of years ago and you complained the whole time,' said Ed mildly as he handed out plates of spaghetti.

'That's because you hired a stupid house out in the middle of the country and made us walk everywhere and Lauren kept throwing up in our bedroom.'

'Only once,' protested Lauren.

'It was at least three times!'

'It wasn't!'

In no time at all the minor squabble had degenerated into a bitter argument about who had been sick when, where and with what degree of inconvenience to the rest of the family.

'Do we have to have this discussion when we're eating?' Ed demanded at last and forcibly changed the conversation by asking Perdita about her time in France.

'Well, I did have food poisoning once,' she said, and the girls laughed when Ed pretended to glower.

'I've heard enough about throwing up this evening, thank you!'

It was just the evening Perdita needed, and she was amazed at how quickly she felt at home with Ed's children. Tom was quieter than the girls, but more than capable of holding his own. Cassie was clearly the dominant personality, but when she forgot her pose of tortured teenager she could be very funny. She and Lauren chattered engagingly about their friends and school, which they claimed to loathe in spite of the fact that they appeared to have settled in with remarkable ease. They were already vilifying their poor teachers as if they had known them for years.

Perdita countered with some of the more scurrilous stories from her own school days in Ellsborough, and they were soon comparing their experiences of being young, particularly the trials of having a strict parent always wanting to know where you were going, what you were doing and, more importantly, who you were doing it with.

'It was like living with the FBI,' Perdita remembered and, sensing an ally, Cassie shot her father a look.

'I know exactly what you mean,' she said meaningfully.

'You know, you're supposed to be on my side,' Ed complained to Perdita with a grin. 'I only invited you because I thought you were a responsible adult!'

By the time she time left, Perdita was feeling brighter and more relaxed than she had done for a long time. The tension that had gripped her when she'd left her mother's house had been swept away by an evening of animated conversation. Supper had been simple but tasty, and although spaghetti wasn't the easiest of dishes to eat elegantly there was something incredibly comforting about sitting around a kitchen table.

Cassie and Tom were made to clear away while Lauren went to get her French homework. Ed watched, resigned, as Perdita did it all for her. Lauren was absolutely delighted to discover that Perdita didn't intend to explain everything to her, but simply wrote out the answers for her to copy.

'I think the idea is that you try and help them to understand,' he tried to point out, but Perdita made a face.

'That's the teacher's job. I'm sure Lauren would much rather I just did it for her.'

Lauren nodded eagerly. 'And now I've done my homework, I can go and watch television!'

'Can Perdita come over when I'm doing *my* French homework?' asked Cassie resentfully as a gloating Lauren gathered up her books and skipped out. 'That's so not fair! Lauren didn't have to do anything!'

'Sorry,' said Perdita to Ed when Cassie had grumbled off. 'Did I cause trouble?'

He laughed. 'Cassie's just jealous. She hates not being the centre of attention.'

'Now, I wonder…' Perdita put a finger to her cheek and pretended to think deeply. 'Is it possible that Cassie is a bit of a fellow peacock?'

'Oh, there's no doubt about that!'

'Poor you, not only having to work with a peacock, but actually living with one too,' she teased and Ed grinned.

'It's certainly challenging…but then peacocks are always worth the extra effort!'

It was at that point that Perdita made the mistake—the *big* mistake—of looking into his eyes and the light-hearted banter evaporated into a sizzling pause.

Tom had slouched off earlier, and it was only now that she suddenly realised that she was alone with Ed again.

While the other three had been there it had been possible to forget that mad moment of awareness when she had been laying the table. She had been able to pretend that her hand wasn't tingling at all where her skin had grazed his, that the sight of his mouth didn't make her feel boneless and that when she looked at his hands her stomach didn't disappear into a dizzy void.

But now all that was back with a vengeance. Perdita's eyes skittered frantically away from his and around the room. 'Goodness, look at the time!' she said on a gasp, and her chair scraped across the tiles as she pushed it back with a sense of desperation. 'I must go.'

This wouldn't do, she told herself, scrabbling for control. There was no way she was going to get hung up on Ed. That would be stupid. She had been through this so many times. Remember what it was like with Nick, she reminded herself. Remember how hurt you were? Remember how you vowed that you would never put yourself in that situation again?

And yet here she was, her throat closed with desire at the mere thought of touching Ed, at the thought of what it would be like to lean against all that solid strength and rest her face against his throat. She had to put it out of her mind *right now*.

Yes, *now*.

Perdita made herself breathe slowly as Ed escorted her out to her car. She could do this. Mind over matter. And her mind was telling her that falling even a little bit in love with Ed was out of the question.

There was absolutely no reason why she shouldn't be a friend to him and his children, but anything more…? No, no, no.

'Thank you so much,' she said, carefully polite. 'I really enjoyed myself.'

'It was a pleasure,' said Ed. 'I'm the one who should thank you for coming. We don't really know anyone here yet, and it's nice for the kids to have some company other than their boring old dad!'

'Why don't you come round to lunch one Sunday?' said Perdita on an impulse. It must be quite lonely for him in Ellsborough, and she had decided to be a friend, hadn't she? 'I'll invite some friends, make it a party,' she added, just in case he thought she was trying to set up a date. 'Bring the kids too. My best friend has teenage children, and they can always sulk together.'

Ed looked pleased. 'That sounds great. Thank you.'

'Well…goodnight.' Perdita hesitated, fiddling with the car keys in her hand. The natural thing now would be to kiss him on the cheek, the way she wouldn't hesitate to do with any other friend. But Ed wasn't any other friend, and the situation suddenly seemed fraught with difficulty.

But what could she do? It wasn't a business meeting so she could hardly offer to shake hands, but getting into the car without a gesture of farewell would seem all wrong.

There was a pause, which she guessed Ed found as awkward as she did, for the moment that she decided to risk a quick brush of the cheeks he leant forward stiffly at the same time. There wouldn't have been a problem if one of them had kept their head still and let the other do the kissing, but as it was they made a complete botch of it and, instead of a demure brush of the cheeks, their lips collided and both instantly recoiled as if stung.

'Sorry!'

'Sorry…my fault.'

For an excruciating moment Perdita couldn't think of anything to say, but she was burningly aware of her mouth where it had touched his. Her whole body seemed to be jangling, and she was very glad of the dim light that hid the colour flooding her cheeks. It was silly to get in such a state about what wasn't even a kiss. It had been an accident, no more than that.

'The French are so much better at this kind of thing,' she said feebly, trying to make a joke out of it. 'You always know how many kisses you're going to get and which side goes first.'

Ed smiled. 'I can't turn myself into a Frenchman, unfortunately, but let's try again anyway.' Stepping closer, he bent his head and Perdita held hers very still as he dropped a kiss on her cheek, very close to the edge of her mouth.

'Goodnight, Perdita.'

Somehow Perdita got herself into her car, started the engine and fumbled with her seat belt. It took ages to get the car into gear, but at last she was reversing out of the drive, raising a hand in farewell and driving to the end of the road, where she had to stop and wait until her hands had stopped shaking enough to grip the steering wheel properly.

Ed had waited until she was out of sight, but he would be back in that warm, slightly chaotic house by now, closing the door behind him, shutting the dark night—and her—out.

It was stupid to feel excluded. Stupid to wish that she could have stayed. Stupid to envy Ed his family when she had never particularly wanted children of her own. Which was just as well now that she was forty, Perdita reminded herself.

Since Nick's rejection, she had accepted that she was probably going to grow old on her own, and she had told herself that there were much worse fates—being unhappily married but afraid to be on her own, for one—and usually she was more than happy to look on the bright side of being single and independent.

So there was no reason at all to suddenly start feeling lonely because she had said that she had to leave, and that Ed Merrick had let her go, closing his front door after her and leaving her out in the cold.

But he had kissed her…Perdita couldn't get the feel of it out of her mind. It hadn't been a *real* kiss, of course, just a brief graze of her cheek. Not what you'd call a *kiss*.

His lips had been warm and firm and sure, though, and she had smelt clean laundry, clean male skin, so close that she was dizzy with it. Had it been deliberate, that kiss so close to her mouth? It would have taken so little for her to turn her head, for their lips to meet.

What would *that* have been like? How would she have felt to let herself lean into him, to part her lips and kiss him back? To slide her arms around his back and feel his warm, solid strength? To be held tightly against him?

It wouldn't have been like being just good friends, now, would it? Perdita's inner voice, the uncomfortably sarcastic one, pointed out, and she sighed as she pulled up outside her flat in a converted warehouse overlooking the river. It was no good, she was going to have to pull herself together about this.

She wasn't quite sure what signals Ed was giving off. Yes, he had indicated that he was ready to move on after his wife's death, and yes, he seemed to like her, and that kiss *might* have been deliberate, but it could just have easily been an affectionate gesture to someone he considered a friend.

And that was how she ought to take it. Because, even if he also had been wondering what a proper kiss would have been like, even if he had hoped that she would smile and turn her face instead of standing rigidly, it wouldn't have taken much for him to realise what a bad idea it would have been.

They had to work together, after all. Much better for him to meet someone outside the office.

Someone who hadn't already discovered to her cost that falling in love with a father meant finding yourself a very long way down his list of priorities.

She would be a friend and nothing more, Perdita decided yet again and, just to prove it, she would invite Millie to meet Ed. They were bound to get on. Millie had teenagers herself and understood the difficulties of being a single parent. And she was a lovely person, warm, friendly and motherly, completely the opposite of Perdita herself, with her 'sharp edges'.

Yes, she would introduce him to Millie, and she would invite Grace as well. He obviously liked her too. Grace didn't have children, but she was widowed, so they would understand each other. Millie and Grace would both be perfect partners for Ed so, by inviting them, Perdita would make it clear that she had no interest in him herself. And, so as not to be too obvious about her matchmaking, she would invite another couple who were also struggling with teenagers, and Rick, who was gay, and excellent company. At least Ed wouldn't feel overwhelmed by women then.

Not that Perdita could imagine Ed feeling overwhelmed by anything. He was too self-contained for that.

In the end, they were to be a party of fifteen. It was a squeeze in Perdita's flat, but she pushed two tables together and spread over a huge cloth to make it look festive. The flat looked wonderful with the early October light pouring in and the sliding doors open on to the balcony.

It was three weeks since she had shared spaghetti bolognaise with Ed and his family, and Perdita had been careful not to seem too eager about seeing him again. Because she was just going to be a friend, right?

Once she had bumped into him when she'd parked in her mother's drive just as he was getting out of his car. Ed had suggested that it might be a good opportunity to introduce him to her mother, and she had done that, which had gone quite well. Otherwise, Perdita had kept contact to work. She was scrupulous about being professional and only talked to him about business, although none of it had helped shake the memory of that brief, impersonal kiss on her cheek.

Which was ridiculous. It wasn't as if he were jaw-droppingly handsome. There was nothing special about him at all, in fact, apart perhaps from those uncomfortably keen eyes, but somehow, once you had started noticing his mouth and his throat and the line of his cheek, it was hard to stop noticing, and, before you knew where you were, a mere glimpse was enough to make it feel as if the ground were tilting beneath your feet and your insides had disappeared, leaving you with that alarming hollow feeling that was much too close to lust for comfort.

All right, stop it now! Perdita told herself firmly every time her thoughts wandered off in that direction. This was getting silly. Ed was her *boss*, a work colleague. She had always made a point of not getting involved with anyone at work, and this was not the time to start. *And* he was a single father, which meant that he had all the concerns Nick had had, but without anyone to share them with. That put him even further out of bounds. Perdita had learnt her lesson.

Or that was what she kept telling herself.

Ed himself had given no indication that he had given their farewell another moment's thought, which just made Perdita feel even more ridiculous. She had pushed a note through his door with the invitation to lunch, reasoning that he could easily find an excuse if he wanted, but Ed had rung her at home to say that they would all love to come.

The sound of his voice in her kitchen had made Perdita feel very odd. She hadn't been expecting it and her reaction had thrown her off balance. She was used to bracing herself against it at work or when she was at her mother's, where there was always a chance that she might bump into him, but not here at home. She wondered how he had got her number but Ed explained before she could ask that it was on the card she had given him in case there was a problem at her mother's house.

Now she was going to see him again. Perdita was conscious of a churning in her stomach that would normally have seemed like nerves if there had been any reason at all for her to feel nervous about seeing a friend. She never felt nervous when Millie or Rick came round, so why feel it because it was Ed? Hadn't she decided that he was just going to be a friend?

As instructed, Millie turned up early on the day of the lunch to help. Her daughters, Roz and Emily, would make their own way later.

'I'm honoured they could fit me into their busy social schedules,' said Perdita as she handed Millie some tomatoes to slice.

'Oh, they'll always make an effort for *you*,' said Millie, pulling off stalks. She reached for a knife. 'I haven't had a chance to thank you properly yet for putting me in touch with Grace. I'm so excited about the job!'

'Is it all agreed, then?'

Millie nodded happily. 'I'm going to start off doing three days a week in the office and we'll see how we go.' She smiled at her friend. 'I can't tell you how grateful I am to you for organising this, Perdita. You've got enough on your mind at the moment without sorting out jobs for me!'

'Well, you know I've always hated seeing your talents going to waste,' said Perdita lightly. 'I know you'll be brilliant.'

'I'm just so thankful for the chance to get some experience,' Millie said with feeling. 'It's hard to get a job when you're over forty, haven't worked in an office for more than fifteen years and never had very impressive qualifications in the first place!'

Perdita was staring into the fridge, half her mind on the conversation, half trying to remember what still had to be done for the lunch, and all of it preoccupied by the prospect of seeing Ed again. 'I get the feeling Grace is more interested in the kind of person you are than in any qualifications,' she murmured.

'She's lovely, isn't she? I'm glad she's coming today.' Millie watched critically as Perdita continued to dither in front of the fridge. 'You seem a bit distracted, Perdita. You're not nervous, are you?' she asked, startling Perdita in the act of pulling out a plate of grilled peppers.

'Of course not,' said Perdita, just managing to stop the peppers sliding on to the floor in time. There was just the suspicion of a snap in her voice. 'Why on earth should I be nervous?'

'Because your gorgeous Ed is coming to lunch, perhaps?'

'He's not mine,' said Perdita sharply. 'And he's not gorgeous.'

Millie received this in disbelieving silence. She started slicing tomatoes. 'So why the lunch in his honour?'

'I'm just being friendly.' Perdita kept her voice carefully cool. 'It's a chance for him to meet some new people, that's all.'

'Because I got the impression the last time you mentioned him that you were quite keen on him,' said Millie.

'Not in the least,' said Perdita. 'In fact, I deliberately invited you and Grace because I think you would get on with him, and I'm sure he'd like you both. You can fight it out between you.'

Her head was bent as she concentrated on peeling the peppers and Millie observed her with a slight smile. 'Well, great,' she said cheerfully. 'If you really don't want him, I'll have him! I think he sounds lovely.'

Perdita's lips tightened slightly. 'He's very nice.'

'I'm so glad now I know you're not interested in him,' Millie went on with enthusiasm. 'I wish you'd told me earlier, though. I could have worn something a bit sexier!'

Sliding a glance at her friend under her lashes, she noted with some amusement that Perdita was looking decidedly cross. She might claim that she didn't care about Ed, but Millie had known her a long time.

'I can't wait to meet him,' she teased, but Perdita didn't seem to think it was funny.

'You're not to embarrass him by being too obvious,' she said tightly. 'I don't want Ed to think I'm matchmaking.'

'Oh, don't worry, I'll be good. But it's OK if I flirt with him a little, isn't it?'

Perdita couldn't understand why Millie seemed to find it all so amusing. Her best friend wasn't usually this irritating, and she was beginning to wish that she had never mentioned Ed. If Millie carried on like this, Ed would probably think that she was too silly for words.

In fact, she was beginning to wish she had never thought of the lunch at all. She couldn't really concentrate on anything and every time the doorbell rang, her heart would go into a frenzy, only to sink abruptly when it only turned out to be Rick or Peter and Jane. Then, when she was sure it must be Ed at last, it was only Grace. By the time he did arrive, her nerves were shredded.

Taking a steadying breath, she opened the door. The Merricks had met Roz and Emily on their way in, so there were six of them standing outside the door, but Perdita saw only Ed, and the sight of him was like a punch, sending the air whooshing from her lungs so that she was left clinging to the door handle for support.

'Hi,' she said weakly.

They all trooped in and the next few minutes were taken up with introductions and getting everyone a drink. Then Perdita had to do all the last minute business with the lunch so she barely had chance to say more than hello. Not that they seemed to be missing her in the other room. She could hear them all talking and laughing and, whenever she went through to put something on the table, Ed seemed very relaxed.

Millie certainly hadn't wasted any time moving in on him, Perdita noted peevishly as she went round topping up glasses. The two of them were nose to nose on the balcony and she had to smile very brightly to show that she didn't mind at all. She had hoped to fix Ed up with Millie, hadn't she? She just hadn't expected Millie to make her interest *quite* that obvious, or Ed to respond quite that quickly.

It wasn't that she wasn't pleased for them, Perdita told herself, but Ed might at least have shown Grace some attention. The fact that Grace seemed to be enjoying herself perfectly happily with Rick and the other couple was neither here nor there.

She took the bottle out to the balcony and refilled their glasses. 'Is everything all right out here?'

'Lovely, thank you.' Millie beamed and waggled her eyebrows meaningfully in a way that Perdita decided to ignore.

'I've just been admiring your flat,' said Ed. 'It's a wonderful location on the river like this. The light is wonderful.'

'I like it,' said Perdita. She wasn't standing that close to him, but she was desperately aware of him. He was wearing chinos and a pale blue linen shirt with short sleeves and she could see the hairs on his forearms glinting in the sun. His eyes were creased slightly against the light, and he looked relaxed and fit.

He looked wonderful.

For a friend.

'I love coming here,' Millie said. 'It's always so calm and stylish, like a haven. My house is a tip—if your teenagers are anywhere near normal, yours probably is too,' she added to Ed, who grinned.

'I haven't seen the carpet for a while, I have to admit.'

Oh, well, if they were going to get into comparing parental horror stories she might as well go, thought Perdita, forgetting that their similar experiences were precisely the reason she had thought Ed and Millie would get on.

'I'll just go and check the rice,' she said with a sparkly smile to show that she didn't feel at all excluded.

'Can I do anything to help?' asked Millie.

If she said yes, Ed would go and join the others, but, on the other hand, Millie would know that was why. Perdita was much too proud to give Millie the slightest excuse to suggest that she might be jealous.

'No, you stay here and entertain Ed,' she said airily instead, but it was hard work keeping the smile pinned in place as she turned to go inside.

Millie watched Ed watch Perdita go and smiled to herself.

'It'll be a fantastic lunch, you wait,' she said to him chattily. 'Perdita is a really good cook.'

Ed transferred his attention back to Millie. 'I get the sense that Perdita is good at a lot of things.'

'I don't know about that,' said Millie, considering the matter honestly. 'She's hopeless at sport or any outdoorsy stuff and, although she's efficient, she's not actually very practical—she's much too impatient. But what she does, she does with style,' she finished with an affectionate smile.

'Yes, I can imagine that,' said Ed. 'You obviously know her very well.'

'We were at school together,' Millie told him, 'and we've been friends ever since. Perdita is the best person I know. She can be a bit prickly sometimes,' she acknowledged fairly, 'but you don't want to take any notice of that. You won't find a truer friend. I would never have got through my divorce without her. My kids have always adored her too. She never talked down to them, even when they were little, and, of course, she can be very funny, which they love.'

'I've noticed that,' said Ed with a smile. 'Mine liked her too.'

'Perdita always gives the impression that she's on top of the world, but she hasn't had that easy a time of it. Her mother's a real worry now, and her brothers are completely useless, just leave everything to Perdita.' Millie paused. 'Has she told you about Nick yet?'

The grey eyes sharpened. 'No.'

'Ah.' said Millie, and left it at that.

CHAPTER SEVEN

ED WATCHED Perdita moving in and out of the kitchen. Her dark hair swung glossily, her brown eyes were bright and that big, generous smile lit up the room. She was wearing jeans with a white shirt instead of her usual bold colours but she was still the most vivid person there. Everyone else looked faintly muted in comparison.

It was hard to believe now that he had found her brittle and faintly off-putting at first. Had he really disapproved of her? He had certainly tried, Ed remembered ruefully.

She was so different from Sue, whose loveliness had been utterly natural. Sue had been fair and fresh-faced with a sweet expression. For someone so pretty, she had had an extraordinary lack of vanity, Ed remembered affectionately. Sue's attention had been lavished on the children rather than herself, and she would never have spent the money Perdita clearly did on clothes or the time on grooming.

Ed had always imagined that Sue was his model of a perfect woman. On the rare occasions when he'd thought about meeting someone new, he'd somehow assumed that he would be looking for someone like her. Perdita was everything Sue hadn't been and yet…and yet…

He *liked* her. This flat was distinctively hers, Ed couldn't help thinking as he looked around him. It exuded brightness and warmth and a stylish, quirky charm, the way she did.

He felt better just being here.

Of course, Perdita herself had made it pretty clear that she wasn't interested in a serious relationship. She had told him outright that she just wanted fun, and she wasn't likely to look to a middle-aged widower like him for *that*!

On the other hand…there *had* been an unmistakable crackle in the air between them at times. Ed could still remember that brief kiss they had shared by her car. It had been so tempting to kiss her lips, to see how she tasted, to discover if her mouth was as warm and generous as it looked, but at the last moment he had lost his nerve, had very properly touched his lips to her cheek instead.

He wished he hadn't. He wished he had kissed her the way he had wanted to. But then, that might have made things awkward, Ed reflected. Perhaps it was for the best. He wouldn't be here otherwise, on their first proper social outing since they had arrived in Ellsborough.

It wasn't just the kids who had left friends behind in London, and they were finding it much easier to settle than he was. Not that everyone in Ellsborough hadn't been pleasant, but when you were forty seven and had a houseful of teenagers and a new job to preoccupy you, it was hard to find the time to make new friends. Ed hadn't appreciated how much he had missed having someone to talk to until Perdita had come round. It would be a shame to jeopardise that.

For now, he decided, he would try to forget about her fragrance and her mouth and the seductive swing of her hair, and concentrate on thinking of her as a friend. Perhaps that would be enough.

Perhaps.

* * *

It was one of the most successful parties that Perdita had ever had. They all squeezed round the table and had to eat with their elbows tucked into their sides. It wasn't very refined but was much better fun than an elegantly laid repast would have been, and once it was clear that there was no option of lolling around looking bored or refusing to eat, the eight kids all got stuck in too. They seemed to have made instant connections amongst themselves, and Millie, Peter, Jane and Rick were clearly ready to include both Ed and Grace in their social circles. Everything was going exactly as Perdita had planned.

Yes, it was a great success. The food was delicious, the conversation animated and the sunshine pouring through the open window. Everyone was enjoying themselves.

Except Perdita.

It took her some time to realise the truth. There she was, surrounded by good friends, all laughing at one of Rick's more outrageous stories. They had scraped the dish clean and polished off the last of the salad, and made her feel loved and appreciated.

Normally, Perdita would have been on sparkling form— probably showing off, she admitted to herself honestly—but today she felt…what?…a bit *testy*, she decided. She couldn't help thinking that she would have enjoyed today more if there had been fewer people, just her and Ed, say, enjoying a quiet lunch on the balcony.

They could have sat close together—close enough to touch?—with a glass of cold wine and watched the river. And when Ed smiled he would have been smiling for *her*, not for Millie or Grace. She wouldn't have felt testy at all then. She would have been…happy. It would have been quiet and peaceful and—

'Ground control to Perdita! Come in, please!' Millie waved a hand in front of Perdita's face, making her start violently.

'What? Sorry?'

'You were miles away!' said Millie, eyeing her curiously. 'And you had a very funny look on your face. What on earth were you thinking about?'

Afraid that Millie might guess the truth, Perdita's eyes slid away from her friend's and found herself snared by Ed's piercing grey gaze instead. He seemed to be able to look right inside her. Oh, God, what if *he* had guessed what she had been dreaming about? That would be a million times worse than Millie suspecting.

There was a constriction in her throat as she made herself look away. 'Oh, nothing really,' she said as vaguely as she could.

'Listen, your mother's fine,' said Millie, apparently misunderstanding the reason for her abstraction. 'You can ring her tonight to check that she's OK, but if she's capable of stubbornly refusing all help, she's capable of managing by herself for a day.'

Perdita seized on the excuse. Good old Millie. Better by far that they all thought that she was fretting about her mother than dreaming about a man she had already decided wasn't for her.

'I know, I should stop worrying about her.' She offered an apologetic smile round the table. 'Sorry.'

'We were just talking about the garden project, as you'd have known if you hadn't been on Planet Perdita,' said Millie. She assumed an air of mock self-importance. 'My role,' she said grandly, 'has expanded already.'

'But you haven't even started working there yet!'

'I know, but Ed and Grace think I should try my hand at

fund-raising. I've already persuaded Peter to promise some sponsorship, haven't I, Peter?'

'Well, I don't know that *persuaded* is the right word to use when my arm was twisted behind my back like that!'

Perdita laughed. It was time she engaged with the conversation instead of drifting off into silly, pointless dreams.

'If I'd known you were going to turn into a ruthless career type, I would never have introduced you to Grace!' she told Millie with a grin.

'I'm very glad you did,' said Grace. 'Millie is going to be just what we need.'

'It's all right for her,' Perdita pretended to grumble. 'She gets to sit in a cushy office, while the Tom and I are out there doing the hard work with the spade!'

'You love it really, Perdita,' said Ed. 'It always sounds as if you and Tom have a good time there.'

'That's what I think,' Millie put in, while Perdita and Tom were still gaping. 'I don't see much sign of her edges getting less sharp, though!'

'How can you *say* that?' Perdita protested, finding her voice at last. 'My edges are so rounded now I'm practically a ball!'

Millie's face lit up with a sudden idea. 'And, talking of balls…why don't we have one to launch the project?'

'A ball? In *Ellsborough*?'

'Well, a party, then,' Millie amended, obviously throwing herself into her new role with gusto. 'We'll invite everybody we know to get people talking about it, and get *The Ellsborough Press* and local businesses along.'

'It's a brilliant idea, but parties cost money,' said Grace doubtfully.

'I know, but I'm sure a company with a sense of corporate social responsibility like Bell Browning would like to sponsor it…wouldn't they, Ed?'

Ed laughed and threw up his hands in surrender. 'I'd better say yes or I'll end up like Paul, nursing a sore arm all week!'

'Thank you!' He earned dazzling smiles from Grace and Millie, and Perdita couldn't help wondering which of them he had been trying to please.

Never had she been so glad to see her guests leave. Her jaw was aching with the effort of keeping her smile in place by the time she closed the door on the last of them. Ed, in fact, had offered to stay and help her clear up, but perversely Perdita had insisted that she could manage on her own.

Now she wished that he had stayed, even if it would have meant Tom and Cassie and Lauren staying too. What was it she had said to Ed? *I don't get lonely.* And she didn't, not normally. She loved her flat but, after she finished clearing up, she sat on the sofa, listening to the silence, and realised that what she had thought was tranquillity was in fact emptiness.

The thought made Perdita feel very sad, but she fought down the tears that clogged her throat without warning. There was no point in feeling sorry for herself. She was the one who had given Nick the ultimatum, so she only had herself to blame when he'd chosen the option she hadn't wanted. It had taken time, but she had convinced herself in the end that independence and self-reliance were better than the constant struggle for Nick's attention.

But they came at a cost.

She was only feeling restless because the party had been so loud and now everyone was gone, Perdita told herself. There were worse things than being alone. But she couldn't help remembering what Ed had said about being married, about thinking about it as sharing rather than giving up.

'Oh, I'm just getting maudlin!' Jumping up from the sofa with an exclamation of irritation, she went to stand on her balcony and look down at the river. It was a beautiful, golden October evening and the water was still and tranquil. People were strolling along the banks, enjoying the autumn sunshine.

Was it just her, Perdita wondered bleakly, or did everyone seem to be a couple or part of a family? Everyone had someone to enjoy the evening with.

Except her.

She shook herself impatiently. It wasn't like her to get down like this. She wasn't a fool. She knew she was only feeling this way because she liked Ed more than she wanted to admit, and the fact was that she hadn't enjoyed seeing him get on quite so well with Millie and Grace.

And this in spite of the fact that she loved Millie and wished she could find someone who would appreciate her and treat her like the gem that she was. Millie needed a lovely, kind, intelligent man like Ed, and Grace deserved another chance at happiness too. If she were a nicer person, Perdita decided darkly, she would be really happy to see either of them end up with Ed.

Evidently she was a horrible person, though, because the truth was that she wanted him for herself, and she didn't want anyone else to have him, even her dearest Millie. But she didn't want the pain and anguish that would inevitably follow, that was for sure. Perdita tested her heart gingerly. It had taken her a long time to get over Nick. She might be feeling a bit sad this evening, but it was nothing compared to the wretchedness of those long months when she couldn't imagine ever being really happy again.

Did she want to go back to feeling that way again? No,

no, no. Perdita's mind reared back in horror at the idea. Absolutely not.

So forget about Ed, she told herself. Sticking with being friends was a good plan. Any more and she'd be risking her poor, battered heart all over again, and this time she wouldn't be able to tell herself that she didn't know exactly how hard it was to fall in love with a single father.

Perdita squared her shoulders. She was a big girl now. She knew what the situation was, and she had made her decision. It was time to stop being such a baby and accept the way things were.

Well, she could do that, Perdita thought, resigned. But she didn't have to be happy about it, surely?

'Have you got a minute?' Ed caught Perdita as she was leaving the boardroom where they had been having the monthly meeting of departmental heads.

'Of course.'

Perdita was on her best behaviour today. This was the first time she had seen Ed since the lunch party on Sunday, and she had had three days to pull herself together and stop being silly about him.

And she had thought it had worked until he'd walked into the meeting and her heart had started springing around her chest.

Still, it was easier to pretend to be cool and business-like when they were talking about budgets and perfor-mance targets and she was armoured in her best suit with its classy little jacket that always made her feel a bit like Audrey Hepburn, although without the same gamine charm, obviously.

She clutched her files to her chest in an attempt to keep

her heart under control as Ed accompanied her down the corridor to the lifts.

'Thank you for Sunday,' said Ed. 'We all really enjoyed it.'

Perdita managed a rather stiff smile. 'I'm glad.'

There was a tiny pause. 'Do you remember that music you liked when you came round to supper?'

'The Bach?'

'Exactly. It turns out that they're playing that piece in a concert in St Margaret's on Saturday. I wondered if you'd like to go?'

Ed felt stupidly nervous as he waited for Perdita to reply. It had seemed such a simple invitation when he had practised it earlier. Music they both enjoyed, a beautiful setting— what reason could she have to say no?

But Perdita was definitely hesitating. She pushed the button to summon the lifts and glanced at him a little uncertainly.

'You did say that you wished that you got to classical concerts more often,' he reminded her, and then worried in case she thought he was being pushy.

'That's true…'

'But perhaps you've got other plans for Saturday night?' he said, hating the false heartiness in his voice. It was so long since he had asked a woman out. Didn't she realise how nervous he was? And how much he wanted her to say yes?

'Well, no,' Perdita had to admit. Afterwards she wondered why she hadn't just lied and pretended that she had a heavy date, but at the time it never occurred to her. Being less than straight wasn't something that came naturally to her.

'Then please come.' Ed threw pride to the wind and told Perdita the truth. 'The girls keep nagging at me to get a life, and this concert is my first step. I don't want to go home and tell them that I fell at the first hurdle of asking someone to go with me.'

When he put it like that, it was hard to say no. And really, what was the big deal about going to a concert with him? It was exactly the kind of thing you did with a friend. It wasn't like dinner, or even a drink. It wasn't a *date*.

Naturally, that didn't stop Perdita feeling pathetically, stupidly, *ridiculously* jittery as she waited for Ed to pick her up that Saturday. The plan was for him to leave his car outside her flat so they could walk into town together. And really, how hard could it be? Perdita asked herself. A church wasn't exactly an intimate environment. They would sit next to each other, listen to some beautiful music, walk home and say goodnight—and she would be ready for the kissing on the cheek thing this time too.

She would keep it cool, keep it casual. Easy.

Typically, the long spell of fine weather had broken in time for the weekend and sullen clouds had been lowering over the city all day, threatening to rain but never quite getting round to it. Her bedroom window overlooked the street and Perdita peered out, to check the weather and not to see if Ed had arrived yet, of course. She had deliberately dressed down in a soft skirt and boots, but she decided at the last minute to pull on a loose cardigan as well and take a coat after all.

Ed was even better prepared. 'I've brought an umbrella,' he said, holding it up. 'Just in case it rains on the way back.'

Having given herself a particularly stern talking-to in the minutes before he'd arrived, Perdita managed the cool, casual thing quite well at first. They talked easily as they walked down the river and then up over the bridge into the heart of the old city.

Ed seemed to be going for cool and casual as well, and

Perdita began to wonder if she had misinterpreted things when he had told her that his daughters were nagging him to get a life. Perhaps they weren't thinking in terms of a girl-friend at all? They had probably just meant that he needed to make some new friends.

Which would be good, of course, because if a friend was all he wanted, she could do that without any problem. That was all she wanted too, and if she was just going out with a friend, she could treat him like Rick or Millie and stop feeling tense.

So why was she still vibrating like a tuning fork?

The concert was held in one of the city's medieval churches, which provided an atmospheric setting and won-derful acoustics. They sat in the old pews, which weren't that comfortable to begin with and got a whole lot more uncom-fortable when someone tried to find a space at the end of the row and they all had to shuffle along.

For one awkward moment Perdita found herself jammed up against Ed's rock-solid body before, with a lot of whis-pered apologies along the line, they managed to rearrange themselves. Perdita felt thoroughly flustered by the brief en-counter and one whole side of her body seemed to be strum-ming where it had been pressed against his. She had thought the time their fingers had brushed in his kitchen was disturb-ing enough, but this was much worse.

She shifted very carefully on the pew. He was still very close. It would take only a moment's relaxation for their shoulders to lean against each other, or their thighs to touch, and that would never do.

Perdita sat rigidly and looked at the worn carvings on the pillars, at the soaring arches, at the frankly rather unpleas-antly hairy neck of the man in front of her, at everything and anything except Ed, who was sitting in self-contained silence beside her.

Not that she needed to be looking at him to picture the humorous grey eyes or the wry set of his mouth. That slight bump in his nose, the way the hair grew at his temples, the exact line of his jaw…Perdita could have drawn them in her sleep, and that worried her. She had known her friend Rick for years and years, but she wouldn't be able to picture him down to the same tiny details.

Once she had known Nick like that, had treasured every tiny detail of him, but now she struggled to conjure him up with anything like the same sharpness. When she thought of him now, what she remembered was the sadness in his eyes, and her own longing and despair.

And now she was sitting next to another man and wanting to touch him with such a fierce need that she felt physically sick. Perdita's gaze skittered desperately around the church, but time and again it would graze Ed's profile in spite of her best efforts not to look at him. Her eyes kept being drawn to the corner of his mouth, to the pulse beating in his neck below his ear, to the severe angle of his cheek.

They were so close. His shoulder was just there, right next to hers. It would be so easy to lean against him and press her lips to his throat. So easy to lay her hand on his thigh. Perdita's palm actually tingled with the realisation of how little it would take to touch him, and she clutched her hands together in her lap, terrified that one of them might reach out for him of its own accord.

Her whole body seemed to be humming and strumming and, much as Perdita wanted to believe that she was uplifted by the music, she knew that it wasn't Bach having this effect on her. It was Ed, doing nothing, saying nothing, just listening quietly to the orchestra as the music swelled and soared up into the roof.

Perdita began to feel quite dizzy with the effort of keeping herself under control, and her mind scrabbled desperately to keep a foothold on reality. Ed was her boss, remember?

He was a single father, *remember*?

She wasn't interested in being more than a friend, remember *that* one?

But it was so hard to remember when he was mere inches away.

When the orchestra broke for an interval, Perdita leapt to her feet before they had all finished applauding, unable to bear the excruciating temptation of sitting so close for a moment longer. 'I could do with stretching my legs,' she said abruptly. 'These pews weren't designed for modern bottoms!'

Since there was no bar to repair to, and the weather was distinctly uninviting outside, they wandered around the church, Perdita chattering feverishly in great bursts and then drying up completely because she couldn't think of anything to say other than, Take me home and make love to me.

The words bubbled in her throat, pressing at her lips until she was in a panic in case they actually burst out of her and she shouted them out loud in the church. At least it would startle all the other concert-goers out of the conversations they were conducting in suitably hushed, reverent tones, Perdita thought wildly. Terrified that Ed would somehow guess what she was thinking, she hugged her arms together and stared at an eighteenth-century funerary monument with ferocious concentration.

There was a stir as the orchestra started filing back in and people headed back to their seats. Ed put his hand against the small of Perdita's back to guide her through the crowd and the last breath in her lungs evaporated at his touch. She could feel the warmth of his palm through two layers of clothing and every sense in her body tingled. She was burning, simmering, *shimmering* with it. Surely Ed could see?

But his expression was impossible to read. He hadn't been flirting, but there had been a smile at the back of his eyes when he looked at her and was it her imagination or was he letting his hand linger on her back longer than was strictly necessary?

Was he?

Perdita barely heard the second part of the concert above the thrumming in her blood and it was a relief to throw her energies into clapping enthusiastically, which at least gave her a chance to pull herself together. Then they got into the business of gathering up coats and Ed's umbrella and shuffling along as the crowd funnelled through the doors at the west end of the church, so she had a few minutes to compose herself.

But it was all wasted the moment she realised that it was still raining outside. On the one hand, it was a very good thing that Ed had been prepared enough to bring an umbrella, so at least they wouldn't get wet. On the other, they were going to have to walk close together all the way back to her flat, and that wasn't good. That wasn't good at all.

'This thing's big enough for both of us,' said Ed, putting up the umbrella and holding it over Perdita's head. 'Come and stay dry.'

Perdita held herself stiffly as they walked back through the city in a charged silence. The streets were slick with rain and tyres hissed as the cars passed them. On a Saturday night there were lots of people around, either going home after an evening out or, in the case of the younger ones, just getting ready to start theirs. They moved in packs through the streets, the girls teetering on high heels and skimpily dressed in spite of the rain.

Ed shook his head. 'That'll be Cassie in a couple of years. She's dying to be old enough to go clubbing.'

'Tell her she'll catch her death if she doesn't wear a nice cardie,' said Perdita.

He gave a snort of laughter. 'I can already hear her reply!'

Perdita was desperately aware of him under the umbrella. Plunging her hands in her pockets, out of temptation, she walked with her head bent and concentrated on breathing nice and steady.

Should she invite Ed in for coffee when they got back to her flat? It would be rude not to, but how was she going to keep her hands off him if they were alone with her single squashy sofa and the soft light of a table lamp and the rain against the windows?

Perdita swallowed hard. What would Ed think if she *did* invite him in? Would he think that she meant to make coffee, or would he interpret it as meaning something quite different? He could always refuse if he didn't want to, she reasoned, and, frankly, why should he? Sheer lust had made her tongue-tied and nervous, so it wasn't as if she had been scintillating company tonight. She stole a glance at Ed's unyielding profile. He was probably formulating a polite excuse about getting back to the kids even now.

But what if he *did* come up? What then? Perdita's mouth dried at the prospect, so much so that the whole question could very well turn out to be academic as she doubted that she could even manage, Would you like a cup of coffee?

They had crossed the bridge and were walking along the river bank now. It was darker down here, but the lamps between the trees cast a wavering yellow light on the dark gleam of water. The river walk was a popular route home for lots of people on this side of town, so they weren't quite alone, but it felt as if they were cut off from everyone else by an invisible shield that trapped them in a universe all of their own where there was only the soft splatter of rain on the umbrella, the muted click of their footsteps and the booming of her pulse.

Absorbed in thought, she was unaware of Ed's gaze on her face. Her skin gleamed palely in the dim light and he could make out the curve of her mouth and the alluring sweep of her lashes against her cheek. Even in the dark, Perdita was vivid, even when silent, there was a sensuous kind of fizz and sparkle about her, as if her body wasn't big enough to contain her personality.

Ed had recognised her verve and intelligence right from the start. He liked her frankness and her generosity and her wit. He thought she was attractive and stylish. But it was only this evening, sitting next to her through that interminable concert, that he had come to realise how incredibly sexy she was and, now that he *had* realised, he was finding it very difficult to think about anything else.

Had he *really* decided at that lunch that being friends would be enough?

Fool, Ed told himself dispassionately. Of course it wasn't enough.

Perdita was taken by surprise when Ed stopped suddenly under a tree, and had gone a few steps out of the shelter of the umbrella before she realised that he wasn't beside her and retraced her steps.

'Is something the matter?'

'Yes.'

'What is it?'

'I don't think,' said Ed slowly, 'that I can go any further until I've kissed you.'

The last of the breath she had been so carefully hoarding leaked out of Perdita at that and she looked at him, her heart hammering so loudly she was sure that he must hear it. The smack of it against her chest wall was really quite painful and she swallowed carefully.

'I…I'm not sure that's a good idea,' she managed with difficulty.

'Nor am I,' said Ed, 'but let's try and then we'll know.'

One hand still holding the umbrella above their heads, he drew Perdita towards him with the other. It would have been easy for her to sidestep him, to pull back, but she didn't. She couldn't resist this deep, dark pull of attraction any longer, and she didn't want to. Just one kiss, she told herself hazily—that wouldn't be so bad, would it?

The touch of Ed's lips sent a strange jolt of recognition through Perdita. It was as if they had kissed a thousand times before, as if she had always known this sense of utter rightness. It was like coming home, she thought dazedly, kissing him back, able to touch him and taste him at last, to slide her arms around him the way she had been thinking about all evening. He felt even better than she had imagined, so warm and solid and steady, his lips so sure on hers, sending honeyed fire spilling through her veins.

Ed let the umbrella fall unheeded to the ground so that he could use both hands to pull her closer, tighter, harder against him. Perdita kissed the way that she did everything else—with passion—but she was softer than he had imagined, softer and sweeter, and breathtakingly pliant in his arms. Her hair was like silk as he tangled his fingers in it, her perfume made his head reel and, as their kisses deepened and grew hungrier, more demanding, Ed felt himself losing his footing and he lifted his head, drawing a ragged breath as he fought for control.

He smoothed the hair back from Perdita's face with a shaky smile, still holding her close in the circle of one arm. 'Well, what do you think?' he asked when he could speak.

'Think?' Perdita looked as dazed as he felt.

'Was it a good idea or not?'

'Probably not,' she said unsteadily, but she was smiling as he drew her back against him and she met his kiss with her own, pulling his head down and spreading her hands over his back, sliding them under his jacket, murmuring with inarticulate pleasure.

CHAPTER EIGHT

IT FELT so good to hold him, to be held by him…Perdita gave herself up to the sheer pleasure of kissing and being kissed, and closed her mind to anything except touch and taste and feel and the slow burn of need. She had no idea how long they stood there under the tree, drizzle dripping through the leaves on to their heads, and she didn't care. She didn't care about anything as long as he would go on kissing her like this.

And then consciousness returned reluctantly to make her aware that Ed had tensed and was lifting his head in spite of her instinctive mumble of protest. She tightened her hands against his withdrawal, but even as she did she heard the unmistakable ring of a mobile phone.

'I'm sorry,' Ed said with something close to despair as he fished it out of his jacket pocket. 'I'm going to have to see if it's one of the kids.'

Numbly, Perdita let her hands drop as he checked to see who the call was from. 'What is it, Cassie?' he barked into the phone.

Perdita's blood was pounding through her body, making her feel light-headed and slightly unsteady on her feet. It was too much of a shock. One moment she had been safe and warm in his arms, the next she was hugging herself against the cold and the damp, listening to Ed's one-sided conversation.

'No...*no*, Cassie...because I don't know any of these people yet...and because you're only fifteen...I don't care, that's the way it is... You're to go home... What's wrong with your legs?... Well, get a taxi...' Cassie's voice squawked in his ear and he sighed. 'Where are you?' he asked, resigned. 'All right, wait there. I'll come and get you.'

Switching off the phone, he turned back to Perdita, a muscle beating in his jaw. 'I'm sorry about that.' He raked his fingers through his hair in a gesture of frustration. 'I'm going to have to go. Cassie's with some friends who are allegedly planning to go off to some party in a place she doesn't know hosted by people she's never met, and she wanted to know if she could go too. She hasn't got any money or a coat and it's raining, and I don't want her walking back on her own...'

He sighed again. 'She was supposed to be staying at home with Tom and Lauren,' he said with an edge as he bent to pick up the discarded umbrella. 'I'm really sorry about this, Perdita,' he said again. 'This wasn't how I wanted this evening to end.'

Perdita already had a bright smile in place. 'Don't worry about it,' she said. 'It doesn't matter. I understand.'

And she *did* understand, that was the trouble. She had been through this so many times with Nick. His children had been younger, but they had had to come first too. Of course they did. How could Perdita have argued against that?

She made herself remember that time with Nick as she lay in bed that night, her body still raging at the abrupt way those kisses with Ed had ended. Time and again, she had made allowances for Nick's preoccupation with his children. Plans had been changed at the last minute, dates interrupted, holidays cancelled as Nick had danced to his ex-wife's tune.

At least Ed didn't have an ex in the background, but it would be just the same. Perdita knew from Millie and other friends how worrying and all-consuming teenagers could be. Of course Ed had to drop everything to go and pick up his fifteen-year-old daughter. Of *course* he needed to make his children his priority.

Of course Perdita would have to accept it. She would have to be the one who always said, *Don't worry. It doesn't matter. I'm fine. I understand.*

But in the end, with Nick, she hadn't been able to accept it any longer. Was it too much to expect that, just occasionally, she could have come first? That he would make time for her, rather than taking it for granted that she would fit in around him and the children? That he would make her feel loved and wanted and not just an extra pressure for him to deal with?

Apparently it had been. Pushed to the limit, Perdita had steeled herself to issue an ultimatum. Give me the attention I deserve or I leave. And Nick had chosen to let her go.

It was just as well Ed's phone had rung when it did, she told herself. Otherwise it would have been too late. They would have come back to the flat, they would have made love, and that would have been it. It would have been impossible to pretend that he didn't really mean anything to her then. And *that* would have been a terrible mistake.

No! cried her body, strumming with frustration. *No, it wouldn't. It would have been worth it!*

But Perdita's head knew better.

So she was ready when Ed came to find her in her office on Monday. He had rung several times on Sunday but she wouldn't answer the phone and made sure that she went out with Rick to get her out of temptation's way that evening.

'About the other night…' he began, but Perdita interrupted him before he could go any further.

'It's fine, Ed. There's no need to explain anything. I understand perfectly.'

Ed was daunted by her bright manner. It was hard to believe that this brittle woman was the same one who had been so soft and warm and responsive on Saturday evening. He had been reeling ever since. There was normally such a refreshing astringency about Perdita and he had been totally unprepared for how sweet she had been, and his body was still aching with frustration

If only Cassie hadn't rung when she had… Ed could cheerfully have throttled his daughter when he'd picked her up. He hadn't, of course, but he had been in an extremely bad mood, to which Cassie had taken exception, and they had argued all the way home, which was *not* the way he had hoped to end the evening.

Now he couldn't stop thinking about Perdita. The memory of her and that startling sweetness was like fire in his blood, and he had longed to see her again. He had been hoping that he could have seen her yesterday, but she had obviously been out all day and he had found himself impatient and nervous as a teenager at the prospect of seeing her today.

Talking in her office wasn't ideal, but surely they were close enough now for that not to matter? Something about her smile, though, was making him uneasy.

'I thought…I *hoped*…that we could try again this evening,' he said as he came into her office and closed the door behind him. 'Cassie's under strict orders to stay home tonight! Have you got time for a drink, at least?'

'I don't think so, Ed.' Perdita had got to her feet when he'd appeared and now she bent over her desk to straighten some papers. The glossy hair swung down, hiding her face. 'I thought about it yesterday and I think it's better if we stick to a professional relationship.'

'You don't think it's a bit late for that?'

When Perdita lifted her head, he could see that her cheeks were tinged with colour. 'I'm sure we can manage to forget Saturday night,' she said with some difficulty.

'I'm not sure *I'm* going to be able to forget it,' Ed said honestly.

Perdita swallowed and hugged her arms together the way she did when she was nervous, and it struck Ed how very familiar she was to him already.

'I don't think mixing business with pleasure is a good idea,' she said uncomfortably, and he thrust his hands into his pockets, trying not to get angry. She was slipping away from him, and there didn't seem to be anything he could do about it.

'It felt like a very good idea on Saturday night,' he reminded her, knowing that he was being unfair but unable to help himself. 'Or are you going to pretend that you didn't enjoy it?'

His voice was harsh and the colour in Perdita's cheeks deepened painfully, but she met his eyes steadily enough.

'No, I'm not going to pretend that, but I do regret it now. I would rather we were just friends.'

'I've got enough friends,' said Ed bitterly. 'I don't want you as a friend. I want you as…'

'As what, Ed?'

He didn't answer immediately. Unable to stand still, he went over to the window and looked out, his back to Perdita, his shoulders rigid. 'You're the first woman I've wanted since Sue died,' he told her without looking at her. 'I think…I thought…that we could have something good together.'

'I'm sorry,' Perdita said quietly. 'I just don't think it could work. Our lives are too different.'

'Are they?'

'You know they are. You've got three children who demand all your attention.'

'Not all of it,' he protested.

'Almost all of it. When they've had the attention they need, and work has the attention it needs, how much would be left for me? Enough for a brief affair, maybe,' she said, answering her own question, 'or an occasional fling. I know, because I've been there before,' she said. 'I don't want that again. I promised myself that if I have another relationship, it'll be a proper one. I deserve more than being someone who just gets squeezed in every now and then between other commitments.'

'I see.' Ed turned from the window, bitterly disappointed. It had felt so good the other night, so right, that he couldn't believe that she was pushing him away.

But he couldn't argue with her. He was hardly going to propose marriage after one kiss, if that was what she wanted, he thought, disappointment feeding an anger that was so much easier to deal with than hurt. He would have to know her a lot better before he could be certain that she would the right stepmother for his kids, even if he was sure that she was right for him.

'Well, there's not much I can say, is there?' he said. 'Except I'm sorry. But of course I will respect your decision. You don't need to worry about me hassling you to change your mind.'

That ought to make her feel better, oughtn't it? Perdita thought. So why did she feel so awful?

'I hope it won't make it difficult working together,' she said awkwardly.

A glimmer of a smile lightened Ed's face. 'Of course not,' he said. 'We're both adults, Perdita. We should be capable of keeping our personal and professional lives separate.'

Easy to *say*, Perdita thought as the days passed. Doing it was another matter. It was very hard when her heart leapt at the mere mention of Ed's name in a meeting, when the sound of his voice set her heart hammering and a mere glimpse of him walking down the corridor was enough to make her hollow with desire.

And it wasn't just at work that she had to be on her guard. There was always the chance that she would bump into him when she visited her mother. She never did, but was constantly on edge in case he appeared.

Every week, she turned up dutifully at the garden project. It made her feel better to know that her colleagues were also required to contribute to the community in some way and, when she heard about some of the projects the others were involved in, Perdita couldn't help thinking that she was better off where she was. She and Tom cleared and dug and dug some more and, although she grumbled as a matter of form, she didn't mind it nearly as much as she said she did. The more often she met Grace, the more she liked her, and it was a chance to catch up with Millie too, who had thrown herself into her new job with gusto.

There was something surprisingly satisfying about hard physical labour too. Perdita dug the heavy clay soil until her back ached, but in lots of ways it was a welcome respite from thinking about Ed or worrying about her mother.

Being with Tom was bittersweet, a constant reminder of Ed, but the closest she could get to him too. Tom was a restful person to work with. He was quiet, uncommunicative even, and the exact opposite of Perdita in many ways, but they made a good team. He might be sullen with his father or at college, but never with Perdita, who liked his quiet sense of humour and the sense of self-containment obviously inherited from his father. If he was still guilty of a "bad attitude" she at least could see no evidence of it.

After the first time, when Ed had picked him up, Tom had to make his own way home from the project and, as she was usually going to see her mother anyway, Perdita would give him a lift. She was never sure if she longed to see Ed or dreaded bumping into him on these occasions. Tom was frustratingly taciturn about life at home so Perdita gleaned little from him, although he did volunteer once that Ed had been in a filthy mood 'for weeks now'.

It seemed that she wasn't the only one suffering then. Again and again, Perdita told herself that she had done the right thing, but she couldn't stop thinking about that kiss down by the river. She replayed it endlessly in her head and even when she managed to think about something else, like work, it was always there, simmering at the edge of her consciousness, ready to flare up into vivid memory at the slightest provocation: the sound of rain on an umbrella, the smell of the river, the sight of Ed's name on a report. Perdita was torn between wishing that she could rewind time to before Cassie's call and congratulating herself on her narrow escape.

'I just wish that I could *forget* it,' she sighed to Millie one evening over a bottle of wine. 'All I want is to not think about it any more.'

She should have been more careful what she wished for, Perdita thought wearily a few days later. Her mother caught an infection that proved stubbornly resistant to antibiotics and she grew alarmingly weak. For the next fortnight, Perdita had no time to think about Ed as she dealt with doctors and ferried her mother to and from hospital for tests.

It was soon clear even to Helen that she couldn't manage on her own while she was unwell, and it was a mark of how ill she felt that Perdita finally persuaded her to accept some help. A carer came in three times a day for half an hour, for which Perdita was enormously grateful, but she still went round first thing in the morning to get her mother out of bed and help her to get dressed. She would try and coax her to eat a little breakfast, and then drive to the office, but it was difficult to concentrate on work and everything seemed to take twice as long as normal.

After work, she went back to check on her mother and spend most of the evening with her before she went home. Perdita felt horribly guilty about not moving in permanently, but she held back from letting out or selling her flat. Some days Helen seemed to be getting better, and Perdita clung to the thought that she could somehow get her old life back eventually.

The tests provided inconclusive and the doctors suggested in the end that her mother was simply at an age when it took longer to bounce back from an infection. Perdita held on to the hope that this was just a temporary situation and made herself concentrate on the signs that Helen was indeed getting stronger. When those were few and far between, though, she would spend the night at her mother's house, sleeping in her old room, and those were the times she found hardest.

It wasn't that she didn't love her mother, but she hated living with her. Their personalities had clashed at the best of times. She was too impatient to be a good nurse, Helen James too old and set in her ways to be a good mother any more. Perdita hated the fact that she was old and ill and resented her for her stubbornness. Too often she would end up snapping at her mother, and then spend the rest of the day feeling guilty.

At least she still had a job, Perdita reminded herself constantly, although she worried, too, that her performance was not as good as it should be. Still, the situation could be so much worse. She ought to feel grateful for what she had.

But as the days turned into a week and one week into two, and she was still staying with her mother, it became harder and harder to feel grateful instead of exhausted and frustrated and dangerously near the end of her tether.

She reached the end of it one cold, wet November evening when she put some of her mother's clothes into the washing machine and helped her upstairs to bed, only to find when she came down again some time later that there was water all over the floor.

Close to tears of tiredness and strain, Perdita rang a few numbers, but it was almost ten o'clock at night and nobody would come out until the next morning. Which meant another morning off work while she waited for the engineer to arrive. Hearing the desperation in her voice, one of them suggested that she pull out the machine and see if one of the hoses at the back had come off. 'If that's the case, you could fix it yourself, love.'

Well, yes, if she had the strength to pull the machine out of its slot. Sloshing around in the great pool of water, Perdita struggled to get a grip of the machine, but it was hopeless and in the end she gave up. She would go and ask if Tom would give her a hand. That wasn't too much to ask, was it?

But it was Ed who answered the door, not one of the children, as she had hoped, and Perdita was horrified at her body's instant, instinctive and quite uncontrollable reaction. It was as if every sense, every nerve ending, had forgotten that she was tired and miserable and was jumping up and down and cheering instead. It was a worrying sign when a month of severe talking-tos had simply left her body overjoyed at the mere sight of him again.

'Perdita!' he said in surprise.

Still smarting from her rejection, Ed had tried to make things easier for both of them by avoiding her as much as possible, but now he was shocked at her appearance. Once his own instinctive leap of joy had subsided, he saw that she was pale and drawn and so tightly wound that she looked as if she would snap if he touched her with his finger. 'What is it?' he asked in concern.

To her horror, Perdita felt tears grab at her throat and for one terrible moment she thought she wasn't going to be able to speak at all as she forced them desperately down.

'I was wondering if Tom could come and help me move my mother's washing machine,' she managed, but her voice was shamefully cracked and wavering all over the place. 'I've had a bit of a flood.'

'I'll come,' said Ed.

Shouting up the stairs to tell his children where he would be, he walked back with Perdita, who was intensely grateful that he wasn't going to ask questions. It would take so little for her to burst into stupid tears, and the quiet reassurance of his presence was making her worse, not better. It would have been so much easier to pull herself together if he had rolled his eyes at her uselessness, or been annoying or patronising.

But Ed wasn't like that. He pulled the washing machine out easily, found the hose that had come off and reattached it without the slightest fuss. Pushing the machine back into place, he turned to find Perdita mopping ineffectually at the water that covered the floor.

'You look terrible,' he told her bluntly. 'Have you had anything to eat?'

'I was just coming to make something when I found this mess,' she said wearily. 'I don't think I can face anything now.'

'You need something or you'll be ill too.' Ed hesitated. 'Why don't you go and have a bath or shower and I'll have a look in the fridge?'

The thought of a bath was so inviting that Perdita had to close her eyes to resist it. 'I need to dry this floor first,' she said.

'I'll do that.' Ed took the mop from her and it was a measure of Perdita's tiredness that she simply didn't have the strength to snatch it back. 'Go on, off you go—but don't fall asleep in the bath or I'll have to come up and get you!'

'I can't let you do this,' she said helplessly.

'Why not?'

'Well, what about Lauren and Cassie and Tom?'

'They've had something to eat, and they know where I am. They're all supposed to be doing their homework, but I have no doubt that the minute they heard I was going out they all sloped downstairs and are happily watching some rubbish on television,' said Ed in a dry voice.

'Still…' Perdita hesitated and he glanced at her.

'Still, what?'

'You shouldn't be doing this for me when…well, you know…'

'When you don't want to kiss again, and have been avoiding me ever since?'

At last there was some colour in her cheeks. 'You said you didn't want to be friends,' she reminded him.

Ed sighed. 'I was angry and disappointed, and I didn't act in the grown-up way I should have done,' he admitted and then he smiled. 'Of course we are friends, Perdita,' he said gently. 'And what any friend would do now is insist that you go and have a bath. Go on, off you go,' he said, making shooing motions with his hand, and Perdita succumbed to the wonderful temptation of being told what to do.

When she came down after her bath, the floor was clean and dry, the washing machine whirring to catch up with its interrupted programme, and the kitchen smelled wonderfully of grilling cheese.

'I've made you macaroni cheese,' Ed told her, seeing her sniff appreciatively. 'It's not very glamorous, but I couldn't find much in the fridge and, anyway, it felt like good comfort food. I've also taken the liberty of finding another bottle of your father's wine. I'm sure he'd agree that you need a glass right now.'

Taking the dish of macaroni out from under the grill, he pulled out a chair from the kitchen table with a flourish. 'If madam would care to take a seat?'

Perdita sat obediently. There was a horrible constriction in her throat which made it impossible to speak but she managed a smile, albeit a very wobbly affair.

Ed set a plate in front of her and presented the dish with a serving spoon. 'Help yourself,' he said.

But Perdita couldn't. All at once the pressure of tears was too much and she had to press her fingers to her eyes to hold them in, and even that wasn't enough to stop the humiliating trickle from beneath her lashes.

'Hey, what have I said?' Ed put down the dish and allowed himself the luxury of touching her. How could he *not* rest his hand on her shoulder when her head was bent so that the dark, silky hair swung forward to hide her face and she was so clearly in need of comfort?

'Nothing. I'm just being pathetic.' Pride helped Perdita draw a deep breath and lift her head, and she brushed the traces of tears furiously from her cheeks. 'I'm just not used to anyone looking after me,' she tried to explain. 'It's only because you're being so nice to me,' she added almost accusingly.

The grey eyes filled with humour. 'Would you rather I was horrible to you?'

'At least I wouldn't snivel,' said Perdita with a return to her old form, and Ed smiled as he pulled out a chair and sat down at the end of the table.

'You're tired and overwrought,' he pointed out. 'A few tears is the least you're allowed. Now eat up your macaroni before it gets cold!' he pretended to scold her.

Perdita picked up her fork. 'This looks delicious.'

'I'm afraid the sauce is a bit lumpy,' Ed apologised with a grimace. 'I can never get it to go smooth. The kids are always moaning about my sauces.'

The sauce was, indeed, lumpy but to Perdita, tired and hungry and desperately in need of some warm, comforting stodge, it was one of the best things she had ever eaten.

'It's fantastic,' she said in between mouthfuls.

'I feel sure you're just being kind,' said Ed, but she could tell that he was pleased. 'You should hear Cassie and Lauren when I make it for them. They get down on their knees and beg me to go on a cooking course where I can learn to make a sauce properly, the minxes!' he finished with a grin.

'You don't need to go on a course,' said Perdita. 'I can teach you how to make a sauce. I'll teach you all, in fact. There's no reason why your kids shouldn't learn, too— there's no mystery to it!'

Ed brightened. 'Would you really do that?'

'Of course,' she said. 'It's what any friend would do,' she quoted his own words back at him.

There was a tiny pause. 'So is friends really all we can be, Perdita?' Ed asked after a moment.

Perdita didn't answer directly. She put down her fork and reached for her wine. 'Did I ever tell you about Nick?' she asked, her eyes on the glass she was turning slowly between her fingers.

Has she told you about Nick yet? Ed remembered Millie's words at Perdita's lunch party.

'No,' he said. 'Is Nick an ex-boyfriend?'

'He was more than a boyfriend,' said Perdita quietly. 'Nick was the centre of my world for two years. I loved him the way I've never loved anyone else. I would have done anything for him.'

Ed wasn't sure that he wanted to hear all this, but he had asked, he supposed. 'I thought you didn't believe in compromise?' he said, remembering what she had told him when they'd first met. 'You must have compromised somewhere along the line if you lasted two years.'

'I did,' she said, her expression sad. 'I compromised everything I believed about myself. I thought I was strong and independent and confident, and it was a shock to realise when I met Nick that I was ready to chuck all of that out of the window as long as I could be with him.'

Ed frowned. 'Didn't he love you?'

'He said that he did,' said Perdita, wondering how to explain Nick to a man like Ed, 'but he was always afraid of committing himself to me.'

'What, even after two years together?'

She bit her lip. It still wasn't easy to think about how

blindly she had believed in Nick, how determinedly she had closed her eyes to what she didn't want to see. It hadn't all been Nick's fault.

'Nick hadn't been separated from his wife that long when I met him,' she tried to explain. 'He still felt guilty about splitting up the family, and he was very concerned about his two children, although they actually adapted to the new situation better than either of their parents.'

'Were you the reason Nick and his wife separated?' Ed made himself ask, and was relieved when Perdita shook her head.

'No, there was nobody else involved. Their relationship had simply broken down and it had all got very nasty—and it went on to be even nastier with the divorce settlement going to court. I understood why Nick was wary of getting married again after that, but I didn't mind. Getting married and having children of my own honestly wasn't an issue for me. I just wanted to be with him,' she said simply. 'And when we were together, it was wonderful.'

Her expression was wistful and Ed poured himself a glass of wine to distract himself from it. He wasn't enjoying hearing about how much she had loved bloody Nick at all.

'What was the problem, then?' he asked, conscious of an edge to his voice that shouldn't have been there.

Still twisting the glass between her fingers, Perdita sighed. 'Nick didn't want us to live together. He thought it might be too difficult for his children to accept me at first, so initially I was introduced as a friend who went back to her own flat at the end of the day.

'The custody arrangements were that Nick saw them one day a week and alternate weekends, but his ex-wife was constantly wanting to change the arrangements.' Perdita's mouth thinned at the memory. 'I'm still sure she was just trying to make trouble between us. She used to go in for a lot of emotional blackmail, telling Sasha and Robin that Nick didn't love them enough, didn't want to see them, all that kind of nonsense, and Nick fell for it every time.'

She shook her head. 'I'd tell him to just ignore her, but he would tie himself into knots trying to placate her because he believed that made life easier for the kids. Maybe he was right, I don't know. All I know is that I was always the one pushed down his list of priorities. You wouldn't believe how often we'd have something planned for the weekend and it would get changed at the last minute because Nick had agreed to do something with the children.'

Ed tried to imagine Perdita meekly accepting the way her plans were continually changed, but he just couldn't do it. She was much too strong a person for that…wasn't she?

But even the strongest people could be vulnerable, he knew, and love made you more vulnerable than anything else.

'It sounds to me as if this Nick was jerking you around,' he said bluntly, and Perdita lifted her shoulders in a strange gesture of defeat.

'He wasn't doing it deliberately, but yes, that was what was happening,' she said. 'And I put up with it.'

CHAPTER NINE

'FOR *two years*?'

Perdita winced at the incredulity in Ed's voice. 'That's the reality of being involved with a single father,' she said, feeling defensive as she always did when she talked about Nick. 'I told myself that I had to accept it. I mean, it was right that he should put his children first. I wouldn't want to be involved with a man who *didn't* put his children first and take his responsibilities as a father seriously.

'The trouble was that those responsibilities took up so much of his attention that there was none left over to deal with his responsibilities as half of a relationship,' she went on after a pause. 'There never seemed to be a time when it could just be about the two of us, and I began to resent the fact that I was the only one he didn't think he had to make an effort for.'

'He was taking you for granted, in fact?'

'Yes,' she said bleakly. It had taken her so long to get over Nick that it was depressing to even remember those days. 'It sounds pathetic when I talk about it now, but you need to understand how much I loved Nick. I couldn't imagine life without him, and so I bent over backwards to be accommodating. I tried to be understanding, and I completely accepted that his children came as part of the package, as it were, so I did my best to help make life easier for him.'

Perdita flushed, still faintly humiliated by the memory of how abject she had been. 'I used to cook and clean and make cakes and do all that sort of stuff in the hope that Nick would start to think of me as a real part of his life but, instead of appreciating me, I think he just took it for granted that I'd always be there doing what was needed. He didn't have to do anything to keep me there. I think he thought that letting me love him was all *he* needed to do—and I let him get away with that for too long.'

Ed was puzzled. Perdita seemed such a strong personality, and her face was full of character; it was hard to imagine her diminished by her love for this Nick, who sounded deeply selfish and complacent to Ed.

'You've never struck me as a doormat type,' he commented and she flushed.

'I wasn't myself. I was trying to be somebody else, somebody I thought Nick would want, but all I did was make a fool of myself. I was always waiting for things to improve, for Nick to be less stressed, for his job to settle down, for his wife to be less vindictive, but, after two years, I realised none of that was ever going to happen.'

'So what was the point when you realised you'd had enough?'

'My father died very suddenly a couple of years ago,' she told him. 'It was a terrible shock. He was always so… Well, anyway,' she said briskly before she let the memories get the better of her. 'My mother's always had a very strong personality too, but she was distraught and it took my brothers a couple of days to get there.'

'So you were holding it all together?' Ed knew exactly

how it felt to be the one who couldn't let go, the one everyone else relied on to get them through the grief and the pain.

'Well…yes…I suppose so,' Perdita remembered. 'I had to be strong for my mother, but I really wanted Nick to be there for *me*.' Pain filled the expressive brown eyes before she looked away. 'I asked him to come for the funeral. I told him I needed him but…'

'He let you do it on your own,' said Ed in a dangerously flat voice as she trailed off, and she nodded miserably.

'His ex-wife wanted to go out and had asked him to have the kids that day and he didn't feel that he could say no.'

Ed looked at Perdita's averted face and swallowed the angry words that he really wanted to say. She didn't need him to tell her what she already knew. How could Nick not have been there for her when she'd needed him so badly?

'That must have hurt a lot,' he said quietly instead.

'Yes,' she agreed on a long sigh, still unable to meet his eyes. The worst thing about remembering that time was how humiliated she had felt. People had kept asking where Nick was, and she had had to make excuses for him, when all she had wanted to do was to shout and to scream.

Drawing a breath, she forced a smile. Not a very good one, but still, a smile. 'It made me realise that he might say that he loved me, but he didn't really. Or at least he didn't love me *enough*. Certainly not enough to show me that he did, or to think about what I needed for once, rather than about what he wanted and needed.'

'Why did you put up with him for so long?' Ed couldn't help asking, brows drawn together in a ferocious scowl.

'Because I loved him,' Perdita said simply, turning her dark eyes to look at him directly at last. 'When I was with him, it all made sense. It was only when I was on my own that I realised that I was making myself a fool for not standing up for what *I* needed, but I was always terrified of losing him. If I thought about life without him, I'd panic. I couldn't even bear to imagine it. So every time I'd persuade myself that he loved me really and if I just hung on everything would be OK.

'After Dad died, I knew I couldn't go on like that. I made myself give Nick an ultimatum. If he wasn't prepared to take me into account, I would leave him.'

Ed tried to imagine how he would feel if Perdita told *him* that. If he had been used to living with her, loving her, and she told him it was over. It had been hard enough when she had refused to see him again after that one kiss.

'What did Nick say?'

'He said it wasn't fair of me to put pressure on him, and that he was too stressed to cope with my problems on top of everything else.' Perdita's voice was empty of all expression and Ed gave a snort of disgust.

'In other words, it was all your fault?'

'Quite,' she said. 'I told him that if he thought of me as a stress, then he'd be better off without me, and I walked away. But it was the hardest thing I've ever done,' she confessed, remembering the anguish she had endured. 'The year after that was the bleakest of my life.

'I know it sounds dramatic, but I really did think my heart was literally broken, I had such a terrible pain inside me here.' She pressed her hand against her chest as if she could still feel that raw grief. 'I couldn't even stand upright properly, the pain was so bad. I don't know what I'd have done if it hadn't been for Millie. She's the one who got me through it.'

'Is that why you moved back to Ellsborough?'

'Partly,' she admitted. 'I was concerned about how Mum would cope, but I hoped that a change of scene would make it easier to get over Nick too.'

'And did it?'

'I think it was probably easier than it would have been if I'd still been in London. I met Nick through work originally, so there was always a risk that I would bump into him again if I'd stayed, but moving made the break harder in some ways too. I had no memories of him in Ellsborough, no hope, nothing to hang on to at all. I just had to start all over again.'

There was a silence. Ed drank his wine, thinking about what Perdita had told him. 'Is that why you won't consider a relationship with me?' he asked at last. 'Because you think I'm like Nick?'

Perdita shook her head. 'No, Ed. You're nothing like Nick. But you do have children, and you do have to put them first. It was a long time before I could think clearly after I left Nick but, when I did, I decided that I was never going to put myself in that position again.' She paused, wondering how to make him understand. 'I want someone who'll put *me* first for a change,' she said. 'I would never ask you to put me before your kids, Ed. It wouldn't be fair of me and you wouldn't be able to do it.'

'So you're only prepared to get involved with a childless man?' Ed's voice was unconsciously hard.

'And there's not that many of them around when you get to your forties—or, at least, not the kind of man you'd want to have a relationship with, I know!' Perdita managed another smile, a better one this time. 'But I've faced up to that. I can grow old disgracefully on my own, if need be. I don't need a man to make my life worth living.'

She hesitated. 'There's no point in me pretending that I

don't find you attractive, Ed,' she said and his head jerked up, the grey eyes alight with an expression that made her heart lurch. 'I do,' she told him. 'But I know what would happen if we got together. We'd go out and Cassie would need a lift, or Tom would need support or Lauren would have forgotten her key…and I'd start to feel resentful, and that would be terrible. Or I might fall in love with you, and my heart won't stand being broken again. I won't let that happen. I…I can't be more than a friend.'

Ed nodded slowly. There was no point in trying to argue with her and, in any case, how could he ask her to take that risk? And she was probably right. His children *were* demanding in ways they would never recognise. Of course there would be evenings that would be interrupted. Ed himself didn't think that was a reason not to try, but he recognised that Perdita had suffered so much after Nick that she was afraid to try again.

It was strange to think of a woman as brave and as confident as Perdita being afraid, but Ed could see how much it had cost her to tell him about Nick. This wasn't just a little something she felt awkward or embarrassed about. The determination not to find herself in that situation again was part of her now.

'Friends it is,' he said after a moment and mustered a smile. 'At least, if we're friends, I'll see you. I've missed you,' he confessed.

Perdita's throat was aching with unshed tears and she swallowed. 'I've missed you too,' she said unsteadily.

'So,' Ed said, determinedly jolly after a tiny pause, 'Millie and Grace tell me the launch party is going ahead in a couple of weeks. Will you be coming?'

'If my mother is well enough,' said Perdita, who had

heard all about the plans for the party from Millie. 'It sounds like it will be a good night.'

A party sounded fun and, God knew, she could do with some of that.

She had almost resigned herself to not being able to go but, as the days passed, her mother recovered her appetite and began to seem so much stronger and so much more like her old self that the doctor talked about the right antibiotics kicking in at last, and Perdita began to think that it might be possible to leave her mother alone at night again.

'Go!' Helen James ordered, making shooing motions with her hands when Perdita talked tentatively about going back to her flat that evening. 'You're making me feel like an old woman, fidgeting over me the whole time. I'm perfectly fine.'

Perdita didn't believe *that*, but it did seem that her mother would be happy to be left overnight, and there was no doubt that it felt wonderful to let herself into the blissful solitude of her own flat once more.

For the first hour or so she really enjoyed herself. She stood on her balcony and watched the river, breathing in the cool, damp air and relishing the quiet. She poured herself a gin and tonic and ran a deep bath. She lay stretched out on her squashy, comfortable sofa and listened to the silence. Her mother always had the television on in the background nowadays and the constant sound had driven Perdita mad. Now she was alone at last and could listen to whatever she liked.

Bliss.

Except that after a while, she began to feel…well, *restless*. Padding into the kitchen on her bare feet, Perdita looked in her larder cupboard for something to eat. The best she could find was a tin of soup, which she opened without enthusiasm and poured into a saucepan.

A tin of soup for one. How sad was that?

She had *wanted* to be on her own again, Perdita reminded herself. She had longed to come back to her own flat and have time to herself. It was perverse to stand here waiting for the soup to heat up and feel wistful as she remembered the evening before. She had gone over to Ed's house when her mother was happily tucked up in bed and watching the television and had taught them all how to make a cheese sauce.

It had been a surprisingly successful evening. In spite of some initial moaning and groaning, particularly from Tom and Cassie, all three of the kids had had a go and the final result had met with unqualified approval.

'I wish you could come and cook every night,' Lauren said, scraping out the dish. 'It's not that you're that bad, Dad,' she added kindly. 'But you've got to admit that the same old things get a bit boring after a while. It would be more interesting if Perdita were here.'

'Sadly for us, Perdita has her own life,' Ed said evenly. 'She's got better things to do than cook for us.'

Did she, though? Perdita wondered glumly as she watched the soup obstinately refusing to come to the boil. At least last night had been fun. Even Tom had come out of his shell and there had been some lively discussions and a lot of laughter, punctuated with a few spats and more than a little shouting on Cassie's part, which had had Perdita and Ed exchanging amused glances.

Yes, it had been a good evening, and Perdita had been sorry to say goodnight and leave them all behind in the warm, chaotic house with the sound of raised voices and clashing music and thunderous footsteps on the stairs.

At least she and Ed were friends again, she reassured herself. It was as if a huge, black cloud had lifted, knowing that she didn't have to be careful any more, that she could go round whenever she liked. There would be no misunderstandings now. She had told Ed about Nick and he had accepted that friends was as much as they were ever going to be.

Being friends was the perfect situation, Perdita decided. No tension, no yearning, no need to touch or feel or taste. Just enjoying each other's company. Just friends. Perfect.

So why, she wondered as she poured soup for one into a mug, didn't it *feel* perfect?

Perdita saw Ed as soon as she walked into the party. He was in a group with Grace and when she saw him smile she felt the familiar longing clench at the base of her spine.

She had never realised that being friends could be so difficult. It had been fine at first. Perdita still thought about how much she had enjoyed the evening she had spent teaching the Merricks how to cook, and she had assumed that things would be settled between them after that.

Only they weren't. It wasn't that anything was said. Ed had obviously accepted her point of view and never introduced anything into the conversation that might be construed as pressure to make her change her mind. Perdita herself was always careful to keep things strictly impersonal.

But there was too much left unsaid. Perdita had yet to convince her body that being just good friends with Ed was enough. He only had to turn his head or smile and every cell in her body started pulsating with a terrible awareness of him. No matter how sternly Perdita commanded her heart to stay firmly in place, the moment Ed walked into the room it would be off, turning handsprings and ricocheting off her ribs until she was breathless and dizzy.

And worse was the insistent buzzing feeling beneath her

skin, the one that said, *Forget friends, put your hand on his thigh, press your lips to his throat, tear off his clothes and kiss him all over—go on, you know you want to,* until Perdita was quivering and fizzing with tension.

Trying not to show it was exhausting. Torn between needing to see him and not wanting Ed to know how much, Perdita became increasingly grouchy and on edge. It was so *tiring* having to be careful the whole time. She had to be careful not to touch him, even by accident, careful not to look directly in his eyes in case he saw how much she really *wanted* to touch him. She had to be careful to think about Nick and how much she had suffered. Careful *not* to remember how good it had felt when Ed had kissed her.

It was getting to the point where Perdita was beginning to wonder if it would be easier in the long run not to be friends at all. Between feeling tense about Ed and worrying about her mother, she seemed unable to relax at all, and she had even contemplated backing out of the party to launch the garden project—until Millie had got wind of her reluctance and informed her that, short of being carted off to hospital in an ambulance, she was most certainly going to attend.

'Your mum's much better—you told me that yourself— so don't even *think* of that as an excuse!' she told Perdita roundly. 'You need a night off. How long is it since you dressed up and had a good time?' she demanded. 'Besides, I need you to chat up potential sponsors and tell them how brilliant the project is.' Millie glanced at her friend. 'Ed'll be there,' she added, studiedly casual.

'I know.' Faced with some very uncomfortable questioning about why exactly she didn't want to go, Perdita gave in and promised that she would turn up.

So here she was, standing at the entrance in a scarlet

sheath dress that she had worn for Dutch courage and a pair of high-heeled strappy sandals that Millie always referred to with mocking coyness as her 'make love to me' shoes.

'You look fantastic!' Millie grabbed her before holding her at arm's length so that she could study her critically. 'That colour is so good on you.' She sighed enviously. 'There won't be a man here who'll be able to keep his eyes off you!'

'Come on, Millie, I'm forty. You know we're invisible now!'

'No way are you invisible in *that* dress,' said Millie with a frank look. 'Or in those shoes, come to that. Who are you wearing them for?'

'I don't know what you mean,' said Perdita stiffly.

'Ed?'

The hateful colour rose in Perdita's cheeks. 'Of course not! I've told you, we're just friends.'

But why was he standing so close to Grace?

'I'm glad you said that.' Millie leant forward confidentially. 'I did want to check it was OK with you before I put my seduction plan into operation.'

'What seduction plan?'

'The seduction of Edward Merrick!' She struck a dramatic pose and Perdita's eyes narrowed.

'What?'

Millie opened her eyes, all innocence. 'Well, you did say I was welcome to him,' she reminded Perdita. 'You're always going on about how you and he are just good friends, so I thought I might as well have a go.' She glanced at her friend to check her reaction. 'Of course, Grace is probably in with a better chance than me. She's beautiful, isn't she?'

She was. Perdita looked over to where Grace was standing next to Ed. She was laughing and her eyes looked huge and luminous in her pale face. A cold hand closed about Perdita's heart.

Millie watched her expression with some satisfaction. You didn't need to be an old friend to see that Perdita didn't like what she saw at all.

'Of course, I can't compete with Grace in the looks department, but it's possible he might prefer somebody with a Good Sense Of Humour. What do you think?' she asked Perdita. 'Am I in with a chance? I mean, you're his friend, you must know what he likes.'

'I've no idea,' snapped Perdita. 'I'm going to get a drink,' she told Millie and stalked away, unaware that her friend was grinning as she watched her go.

Passing a waitress circulating with a tray of drinks, Perdita snatched a glass and practically downed it in one before she could feel her fingers uncurling. The truth was that she *hated* the idea of Ed getting together with either Millie or Grace.

Maybe that would be the answer, though? She considered the matter. Surely it would change things if she knew that he was involved with someone else? Perhaps that was what she needed to stop thinking about him like this. Perhaps then they really could be friends if she knew that the only thing standing between them being anything else was more than her strength of will.

In fact, thought Perdita, downing the rest of her glass, what she really needed was to get involved with someone else herself. Yes, that was it! Helping herself to another glass, she put on her best smile and proceeded to mingle with a vengeance.

She wasn't actually expecting to meet anyone. As she had told Millie, she was getting used to the fact that women over forty were practically invisible, and the room was full of much younger and prettier women. Still, it was gratifying to see appreciation warm the eyes of more than one man, and to discover that, even though she had passed the dreaded four-oh milestone, she could still flirt and be flirted with.

And it was even more gratifying to glance towards Ed and see that he was losing his famous calm and beginning to look positively thunderous.

The closer his brows drew together, the more Perdita flirted, unable to decide whether she was enjoying herself or feeling wretched. The strain was taking its toll on her, though. She was standing chatting with rather forced animation to the director of a local building contractor when she glanced over his shoulder and found herself looking straight into grey eyes she would have recognised anywhere, and something inside her unlocked. It was like being snapped back into consciousness out of a dream.

What was she *doing*? She looked back at her companion. He seemed a perfectly nice, attractive, friendly man, and in other circumstances she might have enjoyed talking to him, but this was now and she didn't want to be with him. She only wanted to be with Ed.

Meeting his gaze once more, Perdita had the strangest sensation that the world was receding behind an invisible barrier. The party continued, people were talking and laughing and lifting their glasses, but the sound was muffled, distant, and there was nothing real but Ed and the expression in his eyes, which had sharpened to a new intensity as she looked back at him.

Then he was pushing his way through the crowds towards her. 'Excuse me,' he said to her puzzled companion as Perdita stood numbly watching him. 'I just need a word with Perdita outside.'

Taking her hand, he practically dragged her to the entrance, where a knot of smokers had escaped and were puffing desperately on their cigarettes. Ed muttered under his breath at finding yet more people around and strode round to the shadows at the side of the old building, Perdita stumbling unresisting after him. Barely out of sight of the smokers, he stopped abruptly and, without a word, pressed her up against the brick wall and kissed her.

It was a furious kiss. His hands were hard, his lips demanding, but Perdita met him halfway, kissing him back as if she were equally angry at the time they had wasted, time they could have been kissing like this. There wasn't even token resistance in her response, only a dazzling explosion of relief that she was in his arms at last, that she could kiss him again, hold him again, run her hands over his back and feel that he was real and warm and solid.

Gasping his name, she blizzarded kisses along his jaw when they broke for breath and Ed gave a shaky laugh.

'God, Perdita, what have you done to me?' he asked in a voice ragged with desire. 'I'm too old to be losing control like this!'

He held her face between his palms. 'You're driving me mad,' he told her between kisses. 'I can't do this any more, I can't just be friends…'

'I know…I know…' she whispered, her lips pressing hungrily against his throat.

Ed gave a great sigh and rested his forehead against hers. 'What are we going to do?' he asked despairingly. 'I can't get rid of my kids, Perdita, but I can't stand not being able to touch you either…I haven't known what to do with myself these last couple of weeks, and tonight…tonight Millie was the last straw.'

'Millie?' Perdita drew back and looked at him with a puzzled frown.

'I think she did it deliberately,' he told her. 'Whenever I turned round, there she was, pointing out how fantastic you look and how pleased she is that you're starting to show an interest in men again after being so hurt by Nick, and had I noticed how men were looking at you?' Ed gave a bark of mirthless laughter. 'Of *course* I'd noticed! It seemed like I was the only one who had to treat you like a friend, and then you looked straight at me and I just snapped... It's a very long time since I've been reduced to dragging a woman out of a party so that I could kiss her!'

Perdita couldn't help smiling. 'Millie's been playing a dark game,' she said. 'She told *me* that she was going to try and seduce you, and no doubt she could see perfectly well that I didn't like that idea at all!'

'She certainly didn't try any seduction. She was too busy needling me about you.' Ed's smile faded as he twined her dark hair around his fingers so he could hold her head still and look deep into her eyes.

'What *are* we going to do? I know why you don't want to get involved with a father, Perdita, but there's more than friendship between us, you know there is.'

'Yes.' Perdita met his gaze squarely. She couldn't pretend now. 'Yes, I know.'

'So...?'

She drew a deep breath. 'So I think we should get it out of our systems.'

'Get *what* exactly out of our systems?' he asked.

'The physical thing...sex,' she clarified with a hint of defiance as he raised his brows in mockery of her coyness. Her eyes were suddenly very direct. 'I want you, Ed. I want you very badly. I've wanted you since that kiss down by the river, probably before, but...'

'You're still scared in case I'm like Nick?' Ed finished for her.

'I'm scared in case any relationship we might have turned out to be like the one I had with Nick,' she corrected him carefully. 'But maybe we could make it easier on ourselves by not trying to have a proper relationship. By not thinking about commitment or forever. By just enjoying the physical attraction between us while it lasts, and not having any expectations beyond that.'

Ed's expression was impossible to read. 'So you'd like an affair?'

'Don't you think it would work? Maybe if we got sex out of the way we could be friends after all,' Perdita suggested hopefully, and he half-smiled.

'I'm not sure it'll be as easy as that.'

'We could try,' she said, willing him to agree. Putting her palms flat against his chest, she slid her hands up and around his neck. 'Don't you want to try?' she whispered, and closed her eyes in relief as she felt Ed's arms go round her to pull her hard against him.

'Is that your best offer?'

She smiled. 'For now.'

'In that case, I'll take it,' said Ed, and then his mouth came down on hers once more and there was no more talking for a very, very long time.

Having *an affair* proved much harder to organise than either of them had imagined. Ed had to take Tom home from the party that night, Perdita felt that she ought to check on her mother every day, Lauren needed to be ferried to and from some netball match, Cassie wanted a friend to sleep over…

'This is hopeless,' said Ed. 'Let's go away for a weekend, where there will just be the two of us.'

Perdita gnawed her bottom lip, desperately tempted but uncertain. 'I don't think I can leave Mum alone that long. I know she has carers during the day, but there are still the evenings…'

'Couldn't you arrange for someone to drop in?' he asked. 'It would just be for a couple of nights.'

'I suppose I could ask Betty.' Perdita thought of her mother's old friend, who was always offering to help. She felt a little awkward about asking, but Betty was delighted.

'It's time you had a break, Perdita,' she said when Perdita mentioned the idea. 'You'll be no good to your mother otherwise. She'll be fine with me.'

'That's Mum sorted,' Perdita reported to Ed. 'What about the kids?'

'Cassie would say that they're old enough to be left, but I don't trust them,' said Ed, resigned. 'There would be a party the moment I'd turned the corner at the end of the road, and God knows what state the house would be in when I got back. Besides, Lauren is only just fourteen,' he said. 'I'll ask my sister if she'll come and keep an eye on them for the weekend.'

'Won't she want to know why you're going away without the children?'

'If I know Joanna, she'll guess exactly why the moment I open my mouth,' Ed said wryly. 'She's been pushing me to get a life for a year or so now, so she'll be delighted.'

It was frustrating having to wait until the weekend, but Perdita told herself that made it a proper affair. This was just how it should be, a time away from their normal responsibilities. She tried not to look forward to the weekend too much, but she couldn't stop herself. She was one huge smile, from the dopey grin on her face to the smallest fibre of her body, swelling and soaring with happiness, fizzing with anticipation and excitement. Over the last few years nothing ever seemed to have worked out the way it should have done, but maybe this time, just once, it would…

When she had been with Nick, the weekends they had planned had so often had to be cancelled at the last minute, and Perdita braced herself for the phone call, but no, Ed picked her up from her flat as agreed on Friday evening and drove up to a pub in the Yorkshire Dales where he had booked a room for two nights. There was no crisis, no urgent message telling them to turn round. Perdita hardly dared to let herself believe that it was really going to happen until Ed drove into the car park behind the pub.

The King's Arms was an attractive old stone building and the pub was famous for its good food. Its spectacular location made it popular with walkers too, and the bar was crowded as they went inside. Not that Perdita noticed much about it. She was zinging with anticipation and her throat was so dry that she could hardly thank the fresh-faced girl who showed them to their room.

The first thing she saw was the bed. The big, wide, inviting double bed where she would be sleeping with Ed at last.

'The restaurant's very busy tonight,' the girl was saying. 'Would you like me to reserve you a table for later?'

'Er…yes,' said Ed, who couldn't take his eyes off Perdita and just wished the girl would go.

'Will nine o'clock be all right?'

'Fine.'

'We'll see you downstairs later, then,' she said with a

smile and—at last—went out, closing the door behind her and leaving them alone.

There was silence in the room.

Perdita cleared her throat. 'What a lovely room.'

Not wanting to look at the bed—and really, there was very little *else* to look at—she walked over to the window, which looked out over a shallow, stony river to darkness beyond. The curtains hadn't yet been drawn and she fingered the tie-back uneasily. The idea of sleeping with Ed had seemed so easy before, but now that they were here, alone, her anticipation and excitement was curdling rapidly into a bad attack of nerves. She was suddenly remembering that she was forty and it was a long time since she had taken her clothes off in front of a man.

Ed came to stand beside her and they both looked out into the darkness. 'It's been a long time for me too,' he said, as if he had read her mind. 'Do you want to wait? We could go and have a drink and a meal and then see how you feel, if you like.'

Perdita took one last look at the river and then turned to face him. Placing her hands flat against his chest, she smiled and shook her head. 'I think we've waited long enough,' she said.

CHAPTER TEN

BY THE time they finally made it downstairs they had missed their table reservation, but they found a tiny table in the corner of the bar where they could sit close together and share a plate of sandwiches, which was all the kitchen could come up with by then.

Perdita was reeling with love, so boneless with satisfaction that she was amazed that her legs had worked well enough to make it down the stairs. Her whole body was throbbing, as if Ed's hands were still sliding hungrily over her, as if his mouth was still teasing, tantalising, making her gasp. As if she could still feel the hard possession of his body and the spinning, shattering pleasure that had engulfed them both.

'This is so perfect,' she said to him when they had finished eating. She was leaning against his shoulder and resting her hand on his thigh, unable to keep her hands off him, wanting to touch him and make sure that this was real. 'I don't deserve it.'

Very tenderly, Ed smoothed her hair back from her cheek and tucked it behind her ear. 'Yes, you do,' he told her, and the warmth in his eyes made Perdita's heart clench anew. 'You deserve everything you want.'

She smiled and slid her hand possessively over his thigh. 'In that case, I want to go back to bed!'

Perdita woke early the next morning. She hadn't slept much—Ed's body was too unfamiliar for that—but she didn't care. She lay pressed into his back, one arm curled round him so that she could feel his chest rising and falling steadily, and her heart swelled. How long was it since she had felt this peaceful, this *happy*?

Outside, the wind was splattering rain against the window. They had never got round to closing the curtains the night before and, by lifting her head cautiously so as not to disturb Ed, Perdita could see…well, not much more than she had been able to see through the darkness. Any view of green hillsides was blanked out by lowering cloud. Strange, when the room felt as if it were full of sunshine…

She lay down again and snuggled closer to Ed, kissing the nape of his neck until he stirred and rolled over to face her. Surprise flickered in his face as he looked at her—had he been expecting to see Sue, and was he disappointed to find her instead? Perdita wondered for one dismayed moment and then pushed the thought aside. This was a new start for both of them.

And, look, he was smiling as the sleep cleared from his face. 'Good morning,' he said, pulling her towards him for a kiss.

'Good morning,' she said demurely. 'I'm afraid there's bad news.'

'What's that?'

'It's raining,' Perdita told him. 'We won't be able to go for that long walk we planned.'

Ed's smile deepened. 'Oh, dear, what shall we do, stuck

in here all day?' he wondered and she gazed innocently up at the ceiling.

'I can't imagine. We're going to be pretty bored.'

He laughed out loud at that and rolled over swiftly to pin her beneath him. 'One thing I never am with you, Perdita, is bored!' he said, and she laughed and wound her arms around his neck.

'I've got an idea about what we can do,' she murmured wickedly.

Afterwards, Perdita was glad that they had that last time of love and laughter together. They were lying lazily entwined in the aftermath of loving, too replete to disentangle, when the phone by the side of the bed jangled.

Ed sighed and stirred reluctantly. 'What's the betting this is them wanting to know if we're going to make it down in time for breakfast?' he asked as he sat up and fumbled for the phone.

'I'm starving.' Perdita stretched luxuriously and ran a hand down his bare back, just for the pleasure of being able to do it. 'If they want us to order, I'll have a full English breakfast and a vat of tea.'

She never forgot the moment she realised that something was wrong. After his initial 'hello', Ed just listened to the voice at the other end of the line. Perdita, watching lazily at first, saw his spine stiffen and she tensed in turn.

'OK, thanks,' said Ed and put down the phone. He stared at it for a moment before turning to Perdita.

'I need to ring home,' he said.

His sister had been trying to ring him, he explained, but he had switched off his mobile phone the night before, so in the end they had remembered the name of the pub and called to leave a message.

Sick at heart, Perdita pulled on a dressing gown and

waited helplessly as Ed dialled home. Please, let it not be one of the kids, she prayed. But why would his sister ring him if it wasn't an emergency?

She couldn't glean much from Ed's side of the conversation. 'Yes…yes…I see…no, you're right…We'll come straight home…' It didn't *sound* like a tragedy but, whatever had happened, the golden happiness had leaked away, the bubble of sunshine had evaporated, leaving just a room in a pub with the rain beating drearily at the window.

Well, she had known it couldn't last, Perdita reminded herself. That was why they were having an affair and not a proper relationship. There was always going to be a reason why they couldn't manage a whole weekend away.

Ed put down the phone heavily. 'What is it?' Perdita demanded, suddenly frightened. 'Is it one of the kids?'

'No,' he said. 'It's your mother.'

Her hand crept slowly to her mouth. 'Mum?'

'It's not as bad as you think,' Ed tried to reassure her hastily. 'She had a fall last night and she's a bit bruised, but otherwise she seems to be OK. Betty called an ambulance anyway, but your mother is refusing to go to hospital. She seems very confused, apparently, and Betty's worried about that. When she couldn't get hold of you, she went to see Joanna, who rang here. Although Betty's with her, they think you're probably the only person who can reassure her at the moment.'

'Yes,' said Perdita in a flat voice. Her face was white but she seemed calm. 'Yes, I'll have to go back.'

Ed was already pulling on his trousers. 'I'll drive you home.'

It was a silent journey back to Ellsborough. Perdita gazed dully out of the window, sick with guilt and bitter disappointment. A great, glitteringly cold stone seemed to be lodged deep inside her, squashing the last remnants of her happiness into oblivion.

Hard to believe now that only a couple of hours ago she had woken and felt as if golden sunshine were pouring through her veins! Now it had all solidified into a dreary leadenness that was weighing her down, making the smallest gesture a huge physical effort. It had all been so perfect…She should have known that it couldn't last.

I don't deserve it. Wasn't that what she had said last night?

'It'll be all right,' Ed said, but Perdita only shook her head.

'No, it won't,' she said. 'It's never going to be all right for my mother again. Oh, she might recover from the bruises, but she's old and she's confused. She isn't going to get better. She's never going to be the mother I remember again. How can it be *all right*?'

Ed glanced at her rigid profile, his own heart sinking. The laughing, loving, vibrant woman who had woken him with kisses that morning had gone, wiped out by the burden of guilt. Was that how she felt about her mother? he wondered sadly. Would he ever see the Perdita he loved again? And he did love her, he knew that now.

'You know, it isn't your fault,' he tried to tell her, but he wasn't surprised when Perdita refused to be comforted.

'I should have been there,' she said bleakly. 'It suited me to believe that Mum was better but deep down I knew that she wasn't. I was just so desperate to get away that I pretended it would all be fine.'

'Betty was there,' Ed pointed out. 'It's not as if you went off and left her on her own.'

'I know, but she needed me last night. It was too much to ask Betty to deal with an accident.'

'Has she fallen like this before?'

'No.'

'Then how were you to know that she would fall the one night you went away?' asked Ed reasonably. 'She could just as easily have fallen when you were there.'

'But at least I would have been there to help her. I should never have gone back to my flat at all.' Perdita's voice was bleak with self-loathing. 'I should have just accepted that she's too old to cope on her own.'

'The doctor said she was getting better. I know she'd been getting a little vague, but the shock of her fall will have made her confused now. There was no way you could have predicted that.'

'All the signs have been there. I put them down to her not being well, but I should have realised that it was more than that.'

'You made sure there was someone to care for her while you were away,' Ed said. 'What more could you have done? I just don't think you should beat yourself up about it,' he added unwisely, and she turned on him, slewing round in her seat belt to face him angrily.

'Oh, really? And what would *you* be doing if it had been one of your children that was hurt last night—if it had been Lauren or Cassie or Tom? If one of them had been lost and confused without you, and you weren't there for them because you'd been off having a good time by yourself?'

Ed made himself stay calm. Perdita needed a focus for her guilt and her anger with herself, and he was the obvious target. 'OK,' he said evenly. 'I probably *would* be beating myself up, you're right—and you would be the one telling me that it wasn't my fault.'

There was a long silence.

Balked of the argument she wanted—*needed*—Perdita turned back to stare unseeingly at the rain shrouding the hills while the windscreen wipers swept uncaringly backwards and forwards with a rhythmic 'thwack'.

'It's not going to work, is it, Ed?' she said after a while.

Ed took his eyes from the road to look at her sharply. 'What do you mean?'

'Us,' she said. 'We can call it an affair instead of a proper relationship, but it doesn't change the fact that we've both got too many other responsibilities to be able to give each other the attention we need to be happy.'

Perdita fought to keep her voice steady, but tears were very close. 'I thought that if we avoided talking about commitment and tried to keep things to a physical relationship it would be easier, but there's always going to be something,' she said, sounding utterly defeated.

'It was my mother this time, but another time it might be one of your kids. I don't mean that they'll necessarily have an accident like hers, but there'll be *something*. They'll need you for some reason and you'll have to go, the way you had to go when Cassie rang that night at the river. We should stop trying to pretend that it can ever work between us.'

'So what are you saying?' Ed was grim-faced. 'That we're both condemned to be alone for the rest of our lives?'

'It won't be for ever,' said Perdita, turning her face away so he wouldn't see the despair in her eyes. 'Your children will grow up and leave home.' She took a breath. 'My mother will die,' she went on, accepting it for the first time, 'but that isn't going to happen yet. It's just bad timing for us, Ed,' she tried to explain. 'Maybe we'll both meet someone else when we're not overwhelmed by our responsibilities, the way we are now. I hope so. It's just…not now.'

'What about last night?' he asked more harshly than he

had intended. 'What about this morning? Are you just going to pretend that never happened?'

There was a raw ache at the back of Perdita's throat, pressing behind her eyes and across the bridge of her nose, too painful for the release of tears.

'No,' she said unsteadily. 'No, I'll always keep our time there as a wonderful memory. It was like a dream, being able to run away and forget about everyone else, but you can't live like that the whole time. That's not how real life works. In real life we just have to get on with what we have to do. You have to look after your family. I have to look after my mother. That's the way it is.'

She paused and, when she spoke again, her voice cracked. 'I'm sorry, Ed.'

'I'm sorry too.'

Ed wanted to shout at her, to shake her. He wanted to refuse to let her do this, but there was no point in trying to talk to Perdita then. She was too consumed by worry and guilt to think clearly.

And, after all, might she have a point? he wondered bitterly. He couldn't pretend that his responsibilities didn't exist any more than she could. Was she right in thinking that there would be too many obstacles to finding time to be together? Ever since Sue's death, he had focused on the need to concentrate on his children, to try and be both parents to them, and that took time. What was different now?

Perdita was the difference, thought Ed. He had let himself like her, and then he had let himself love her, and now she was slipping through his fingers and there wasn't a damned thing he could do about it. He couldn't force her not to worry about her mother, and how could he promise that he would never worry about the kids? She wouldn't believe him even if he did.

Did that mean that he had to accept losing Perdita, then, and be content, like her, with a wonderful memory?

Perdita stuck her fork in the ground and put a hand to her aching back as she straightened and paused for breath.

Quarter to four. It was almost dark. There was little enough light on a December afternoon as it was, and even less on a day like today when the grey clouds pressed like a thick, impenetrable blanket over the city, seeping rain and depression. Perdita squinted upwards. It was impossible to believe on a day like this that above the clouds the sky would be clear and blue. It seemed a very long time since the sun had beaten its way through the cloud cover to shine on Ellsborough.

Not since she had excitedly planned her weekend away with Ed. Maybe the weather hadn't really been perfect then either, but she remembered feeling as if the sun was pouring down on her, pouring its golden brilliance through her, warming her and lightening her and filling her with its radiance.

It felt like a lifetime ago. Perdita could feel her face starting to crumple at the memory and she scowled ferociously to stop the tears. Grabbing the fork once more, she pushed it deep into the earth with her foot and hoisted up a great clod, wishing that she could dig out the pain that easily.

She had taken to spending as much time as she could at the garden project, which was beginning, very slowly, to take shape just as Grace had promised. Once all the rubbish had been cleared away, they had started to lay out planting areas, all of which had to be dug over until they were clear of the worst of the stones and weeds.

Perdita found it easier to dig than to think, and she often came, like today, at a weekend. Strictly speaking, she only needed to spend a couple of hours a week there, but she liked it when there was no one else around and she could dig and dig and dig until she was so tired that it blanked everything else out. At the bleakest, blackest times—and there were lots of those—it was the only thing that helped her through the days.

Her mother had recovered from her bruises eventually, but the shock of her fall seemed to have had a more lingering effect. She was much more confused now and the good days when she was alert and almost her old self were getting further and further apart.

It was breaking Perdita's heart to see her mother slithering and sliding unstoppably into dementia. That terrible day when she had arrived back with Ed, Helen James had clutched at her as if Perdita were her only anchor in a muddled, nightmarish world—as perhaps she was. Their roles were completely reversed now. It was Perdita's turn to offer care and comfort and calm while her mother grew increasingly helpless.

Having successfully introduced the idea of carers when Helen had been unwell with her infection, Perdita could have arranged for twenty-four hour cover, but she had put her flat on the market anyway. Partly, it was a penance for being away when her mother had needed her most, but it was also a practical move. Even part-time care at home was very expensive and there was no way Perdita could afford it long-term unless one of their properties was sold. She knew how much it had always meant to Helen to stay in her own home. If that was all she could do for her now, so be it, Perdita had decided. She couldn't leave her mother now, in any case, so she might as well move back and be on hand for as long as she was needed.

The only problem was being so close to Ed. It was bad

enough at work, although Perdita was well aware that he was making things as easy for her as possible by keeping meetings to an absolute minimum. She suspected, too, that he had authorised all the support that she was getting from Human Resources, with as much time off as she needed to sort out her mother's care.

She rarely saw him now and, when she did, every glimpse was agony—and all she had to live for at the same time.

Sometimes Perdita wondered whether she should think about changing jobs, but she simply couldn't cope with upheaval at work on top of everything else. Not that she could imagine anyone offering her a job at the moment. She felt beaten and bedraggled and her confidence was as low as her spirits.

In any case, a new job wouldn't help. As long as her mother was alive, she would be living next door to Ed, with all the desperate longing and the painful memories that involved. She would just have to get used to the leap of her heart when she saw his car in the drive, Perdita told herself. She would have to accept that her eyes would jerk to the window whenever she heard the slam of his front door in case it was Ed, would have to fight the constant temptation of running out to him and throwing herself at him, just so that she could touch him, feel him, again.

It was impossible not to be aware of the comings and goings next door. There were frequent arguments conducted at the top of Cassie's voice, followed by much slamming and stomping, and Perdita wondered how Ed was coping with it all.

Did he feel as lonely as she did? Did he ache with loss at the thought of what they had almost had, when it had seemed possible that they could have everything and be happy? Did he torture himself remembering every second of the night they had spent together, by imagining how things might have been if the phone had never rung that day, if her mother had never fallen…?

But what was the point of wondering that? Perdita told herself miserably. If not then, it would have been another day, there would have been another incident. It would never have worked.

Oh, God, now she was crying again! Furiously, Perdita blinked her tears away. There was no point in self-pity.

She shoved the fork into the earth once more. Push, bend, lift. Push, bend, lift. Don't think about anything else. Just dig.

She had another half hour before she needed to be home to relieve the afternoon carer, and she could get this whole bed done if she stopped being pathetic and went for it. She might as well have *something* to show for her miserable afternoon in the rain.

Perdita was so intent on digging that she didn't notice the figure approaching through the gloom until a pair of muddy boots and a fork appeared beneath her gaze and she jerked her head up, startled, to find Ed standing right before her.

Ed. She froze, her heart ballooning with a curious mixture of joy and dismay. She had longed and dreaded being this close to him again and, now that the moment was here, all she could do was stare hungrily at him and feel truly alive for the first time in three weeks.

He was wearing a faded old jacket. Drizzle clung to his hair and eyelashes and he looked tired and strained. He looked wonderful. He was here.

Very slowly, Perdita straightened, clutching on to her fork as if it were her last hope of sanity. Every nerve in her body was urging her to smile and smile and launch herself into his arms, while every cell in her brain shrieked caution.

Don't let yourself hope it will be all right. Don't put yourself through it all again.

'Ed…' she said at last on a long, wavering breath. 'What are you doing here?'

'Looking for you,' he said, sounding so normal, so much himself, that Perdita's heart cracked with longing. 'Millie told me you would be here.' He lifted the fork with an ironic smile. 'She even gave me this and told me to make myself useful.'

He plunged the fork into the ground and started to dig next to Perdita. 'What's going to be planted here?'

'Alliums and irises and tulips, Grace says.' Perdita's voice sounded as if it was coming from someone else entirely. 'It's hard to believe at the moment, but the way she describes it, it should be beautiful. We've got a lot of hard work to do before then, though.'

'Anything worth having is worth working for,' said Ed. He glanced up at her as he dug. 'Even if it's hard going to begin with, with a little effort, a little nourishing, you get something beautiful in the end. Don't you agree?'

'Are we still talking about gardening?' asked Perdita after a tiny pause, and he laughed.

'No, I thought you would like my little metaphor, though. You know, a relationship is like a garden—you have to plant it, fertilise it, prune it, and all that other stuff if you want it to flourish.'

'I think that metaphor's been used before,' she said a little tartly.

Ed smiled one of his rare, startling smiles and then his face grew serious. 'I've missed you, Perdita,' he said in a quiet voice.

Perdita didn't say anything. She was too afraid that she would start to cry and tell him how desperately, desperately she had missed him too. She started digging again instead and concentrated on swallowing the great stone in her throat.

Side by side, they dug in silence. 'How have you been?' Ed asked at last.

'All right,' she lied. 'And you?'

He shook his head. 'I haven't been all right,' he said. 'I've been in a bad way.'

The desolation in his voice made Perdita falter in her digging. 'I'm sorry, Ed,' she whispered.

'I don't want you to be sorry,' said Ed. 'I want you to change your mind.'

'I…can't,' she said in anguish.

'Why *not*?' Thrusting his fork into the earth in his frustration, Ed searched for the right words. 'I've tried to accept your decision, Perdita,' he said at last. 'I thought about what you said. I even wondered if you were right. But I can't believe that you are,' he told her. 'You said we'd have to accept being alone while we had responsibilities, but I've realised that I don't want to be alone.'

He stopped and shook his head. 'No, that's wrong. What I mean is, I don't want to be without *you*. I don't want someone who doesn't have a parent or a kid or a dog or a demanding job to distract her, even if such a person exists. I only want you,' he finished simply.

'Ed…' Perdita began helplessly, not even sure how she would go on, but he overrode her anyway.

'I've been married, Perdita. I know how good it can be when there's someone there beside you, someone who'll stick with you, cry with you, laugh with you, celebrate with you, mourn with you…*love* with you.'

Ed paused. 'I loved Sue,' he said quietly. 'Nothing is going to change that, but I love you too, and I need you and I want you beside me to do all that crying and laughing and loving and everything else again. I want us to do them together.'

'You've still got the kids,' Perdita reminded him. She was trembling, holding on to her fork with a kind of desperation, trying to hold on to all the reasons why she knew it could never work between them... What were they again?

'Yes, I've still got the kids,' Ed agreed, 'but they don't change the way I feel about you.'

Reaching for Perdita's fork, he shoved it into the ground next to his own and very deliberately drew off her bulky gardening gloves so that he could take hold of her hands.

'I know Nick hurt you, Perdita, but his isn't the only way of loving.' His fingers were very warm and indescribably comforting as they curled around hers. 'It seems to me that you can't put a ranking on love. I can't say that I love Cassie more than Lauren, or Lauren more than Tom, or you more or less than Sue. You're all the same. You're all in my heart.'

His hands tightened around hers. 'There's room for all of you. The question is, have you got room in your heart for all of us?'

Perdita's dark eyes were shimmering with unshed tears. 'You know there is,' she said brokenly. 'I do love you, Ed. I love you more than I could have thought possible and I've missed you every second since we came back from Burnham, but you deserve so much more than I can give you at the moment.'

'More than what?' he asked gently.

'More than a few moments between working and caring for my mother.' Perdita swallowed the lump in her throat. 'There's nothing else in my life at the moment. I can't just abandon Mum, or put her in a home, but how can I give you what you need when I'm looking after her?'

Ed looked down into her face. Raindrops spangled her dark hair and her eyes were huge and shining in the gathering dusk.

'You can give me what I need just by being there,' he told her slowly. 'Yes, you may have to drop everything sometimes if your mother needs you. Yes, we may have to cut short a dinner or cancel a date because of one of the kids, but it won't always happen that way. And when I come back from ferrying Cassie to a party, you'll be there for me, just like I'll be there for you when you've had a hard day coping with your mother.'

He drew her closer. 'You're too used to assuming that you have to do everything on your own, Perdita. You don't. I'll help you and you can help me, because God knows I'm going to need help with Cassie and Lauren over the next few years!'

Perdita's heart was pounding with hope and she smiled waveringly. 'I've heard some of the rows.'

'Then you'll know that it's not going to be easy,' said Ed with a smile before his expression grew serious again. 'Do you remember the bar at Burnham?'

'When I said everything was perfect?'

He nodded. 'It won't be perfect, Perdita. It will be hard. There aren't going to be any magic solutions, you were right about that. Your mother isn't going to get better. The kids aren't going to suddenly become polite and helpful and bored with partying. They aren't going to switch off the television voluntarily and do their homework without nagging…and they aren't going to forgive me if I don't find a way of persuading you to marry us.'

Perdita was betrayed into a laugh. 'Us? Would I be marrying all of you?'

'I'm afraid so.' A smile that started at the back of Ed's

eyes was spreading over his face. 'You'd be marrying the whole package: me, Tom, Cassie and Lauren, just as I'd be marrying you and your mother.'

Releasing her hands at last, he cupped her face between his palms. 'We can find a way of managing things together, Perdita. Marry me, and come and live with us. Sell your flat and pay for twenty four hour care for your mother. It's what she needs now, and it doesn't mean that you can't be there for her. She can stay in her house and you can see her every day. And if you can't for any reason, then you and she will have a whole family who can help. If you're away working, I'll go and see her, and if we're both away, the kids will check that she's OK. That's what families are for. We can do anything as long as we're together.'

He made it seem so easy. He sounded so certain, and she felt so safe between his hands. 'Do you really think it could work?' Perdita asked, wanting—longing—to believe him, but not daring to.

'We won't know unless we try,' said Ed.

'And how do we do that?'

'We stick together. We love each other. We support each other the best way we can.' His hands slid over her wet shoulders and down her arms to pull her closer. 'We don't have expectations that it will be perfect. We just take each day as it comes and be glad that we have each other.'

He smiled down at her, but she could see the anxiety in his eyes, as if he still wasn't sure of her. 'What do you think?

Heedless of the drizzle, Perdita gazed back at him as the certainty and the happiness began to trickle back into her sore heart. 'I think…' she began in a voice that wobbled ridiculously with emotion. 'I think it would be wonderful if we could do that.'

'So will you try with me?'

'Yes.' She smiled at him through her tears as she reached for him. 'Oh, yes, I will!'

Ed's arms came round her then and he held her hard against him. 'And you'll marry me?' he asked urgently, tipping her face up to his.

'Only if I get the whole package,' said Perdita. 'Only if I get to marry Tom and Cassie and Lauren too,' she said, and he then kissed her at last.

The drizzle quickened into rain as they kissed and kissed and kissed some more, but neither Ed nor Perdita noticed, and when they ran out of breath they just held each other tight, thinking how close they had come to letting it all go.

It was some time before Ed realised that there was water trickling down his neck and he held out his hand, squinting up at the rain. 'We're getting soaked here. Let's go and find somewhere drier where I can kiss you.'

Perdita clapped a hand to her mouth as reality flooded belatedly back. 'What time is it? I said I'd be back before Mum's carer leaves at four thirty.'

'It looks as if we'd better go and get dry there then, doesn't it?' said Ed, glancing at his watch.

Stacking away the forks safely, they ran for the shelter of Ed's car. Perdita smiled ruefully as Ed started the engine.

'It's starting already, isn't it?' she said, squeezing the worst of the rain out of her hair. 'Fitting in with each other's responsibilities?'

But Ed only smiled. 'That's the way it's going to be,' he said. 'We're starting a new life, aren't we? We may as well start the way we mean to go on.'

'Together?' asked Perdita, and he leaned over to kiss her,

a kiss so indescribably sweet and intense and so full of promise that her heart sang.

'Yes,' he said. 'Together.'

HARLEQUIN

More Than Words

"Changing lives stride by stride— I did it my way!"

—Jeanne Greenberg, real-life heroine

Jeanne Greenberg is a Harlequin More Than Words
award winner and the founder of SARI Therapeutic Riding.

Discover your inner heroine!

REQUEST YOUR FREE BOOKS!
2 FREE NOVELS PLUS 2
FREE GIFTS!

HARLEQUIN ROMANCE®

From the Heart, For the Heart

YES! Please send me 2 FREE Harlequin Romance® novels and my 2 FREE gifts. After receiving them, if I don't wish to receive any more books, I can return the shipping statement marked "cancel." If I don't cancel, I will receive 4 brand-new novels every month and be billed just $3.57 per book in the U.S., or $4.05 per book in Canada, plus 25¢ shipping and handling per book and applicable taxes, if any*. That's a savings of over 15% off the cover price! I understand that accepting the 2 free books and gifts places me under no obligation to buy anything. I can always return a shipment and cancel at any time. Even if I never buy another book from Harlequin, the two free books and gifts are mine to keep forever.

114 HDN EEV7 314 HDN EEWK

Name	(PLEASE PRINT)

Address	Apt.

City	State/Prov.	Zip/Postal Code

Signature (if under 18, a parent or guardian must sign)

Mail to the **Harlequin Reader Service®**:
IN U.S.A.: P.O. Box 1867, Buffalo, NY 14240-1867
IN CANADA: P.O. Box 609, Fort Erie, Ontario L2A 5X3

Not valid to current Harlequin Romance subscribers.

Want to try two free books from another line?
Call 1-800-873-8635 or visit www.morefreebooks.com.

* Terms and prices subject to change without notice. NY residents add applicable sales tax. Canadian residents will be charged applicable provincial taxes and GST. This offer is limited to one order per household. All orders subject to approval. Credit or debit balances in a customer's account(s) may be offset by any other outstanding balance owed by or to the customer. Please allow 4 to 6 weeks for delivery.

Your Privacy: Harlequin is committed to protecting your privacy. Our Privacy Policy is available online at www.eHarlequin.com or upon request from the Reader Service. From time to time we make our lists of customers available to reputable firms who may have a product or service of interest to you. If you would prefer we not share your name and address, please check here. ☐

The Taken

Tierney Doyle is used to being criticized for
her psychic abilities, yet the tough-as-nails—
and drop-dead-gorgeous—detective has no doubt
about what she has uncovered in the case of a
string of unsolved murders. And Tierney is slowly
discovering that working so close to her partner,
detective Wade Callahan, could be lethal.

Look for

Danger Signals
by Kathleen Creighton

Available in April wherever books are sold.

Coming Next Month

Spring is in the air this month with brides, babies and single dads, and the start of two new can't-miss series: *The Wedding Planners* and *A Bride for All Seasons.*

#4015 WEDDING BELLS AT WANDERING CREEK RANCH
Patricia Thayer
Western Weddings
Dark, brooding detective Jack allows no one to get close—until he takes on stunning Willow's case. His head tells him to run a mile, but will he listen to his heart instead?

#4016 THE BRIDE'S BABY Liz Fielding
A Bride for All Seasons
Events manager Sylvie Smith has been roped into pretending to be a bride for a wedding fair—but she's five months pregnant, and the father doesn't know yet! Then she comes face-to-face with him...and his eyes are firmly fixed on her bump.

#4017 SWEETHEART LOST AND FOUND Shirley Jump
The Wedding Planners
The first book of the sparkling series in which six women who plan perfect weddings find their own happy endings. Florist Callie made a mistake years ago and let a good man go. Now she keeps her heart safe. But the good man is back, and Callie might just get a second chance!

#4018 EXPECTING A MIRACLE Jackie Braun
Baby on Board
Pregnant and alone, Lauren moves to the perfect place for her soon-to-be family of two. Then she's blindsided by her anything-but-maternal attraction to her sexy new landlord, Gavin!

#4019 THE SINGLE DAD'S PATCHWORK FAMILY Claire Baxter
Being a single parent is hard, especially when there's been heartache in the past. Chase had planned to raise his daughter alone. But then he meets single mum Regan, and the pieces start falling together again.

#4020 THE LONER'S GUARDED HEART Michelle Douglas
Heart to Heart
Josie's longed-for holiday is in a cabin in an isolated Australian idyll. Her only neighbor for miles is the gorgeous but taciturn Kent Black, who has cut himself off from the world. And Josie can't help but be intrigued....

HRCNM0308